"*Black Out The Stars* shows you that there is a reason you were afraid of that cellar as a child. A visceral, haunting novel about generational secrets that'll stay long in your mind."

-Erika T. Wurth, author of *White Horse* and *The Haunting of Room 904*

"Christopher Bond has crafted a pond scum gothic that reeks of ghosts and regret. Hold your breath before diving into *Black Out The Stars*. It might be your last."

- Clay McLeod Chapman, author of *Wake Up and Open Your Eyes*

"A deep, dark haunting told in an engaging narrative style. Chris Bond brings grief and heartache to life and sets the stage for the reveal of a dreadful family secret. Well paced and beautifully drawn, *Black Out The Stars* is an eeric, delicious read from start to finish."

- Laurel Hightower, author of *The Day of the Door*

BLACK OUT THE STARS

ALSO BY
CHRISTOPHER BOND

THE DEVIL CAME DOWN THE MOUNTAIN

BLACK OUT THE STARS

A NOVEL

CHRISTOPHER BOND

Copyright © 2025 by Third Estate Books
Copyright of individual works is maintained by the author.
All rights reserved. No part of this book may be reproduced or used in any manner without written permission of the copyright owner except for the use of quotations in a book review.

Edited by Jacy Morris
Cover Art & Design by Todd Keisling | Dullington Design Co.
Interior formatting by Katherine Silva

ISBN (Paperback): 979-8-9868455-9-3
ISBN (Digital online): 979-8-9868455-8-6
First paperback edition: March 2025
Published by Third Estate Books
https://www.thirdestatebooks.com

This book is dedicated to my mother, Cynthia Louise, who moved our family to Hilborn when I was seven years old.

And to my sisters, Jennifer and Jami, who helped me survive it.

CHAPTER ONE

Can a house be a ghost? Can a place?

I've been asking myself that a lot lately. And I'm not talking about *haunted houses*, either, at least not the ones you see in movies or read about in a Stephen King novel. Empty rooms filled with spirits, benign or malevolent or both, trapped in this life like poisonous gasses in the depths of collapsed mines. Rattling chains and spiderwebs. Squeaky doors and shadows as black as panther fur. All that other cliché shit. No, I'm not talking about that. But can a house itself be the ghost? When I pulled into the gravel driveway that led to the little two-story farmhouse out on Crayton Road, it felt like that, like I was seeing a ghost made whole, unmoved and unafraid to show itself in the light of day.

It wasn't haunted; I could feel that in my bones.

It was the thing that haunts.

I pulled my Forester slowly down the long driveway, the gravel crunching and popping under the tires like the bones of small animals. The stalks of corn to either side stood at attention like an honor guard as I drifted by, their drying leaves rasping in the gentle breeze, a chorus of scratchy whispers announcing my arrival. *He made it back*, they seemed to be murmuring. *He's home.* Home, yeah. Not that this house—The Roost, we called it—had ever been my home. But it was still home in its way. The place where my family began. The spot of earth staked out by my great-great-grandpa James when he'd traveled west from Philadelphia a century before. An unassuming two-acre lot just outside Hilborn, Ohio, smack dab in the middle of the Rust Belt. Fertile soil to raise animals and to grow crops, and, yes, to grow a family.

Other things grew there, too, but I didn't know that then.

I pulled up behind the brown pickup with the sun-weathered *Castle Construction* decal on the side and parked in front of the house. Up close, the place didn't seem that sinister; in fact, it seemed like it was barely holding itself together. It had been updated with white vinyl siding sometime in the 80s, but little else had changed in the 120-odd years since Grandpa James had raised the first beams with the help of a few neighbors. It was small compared to modern houses, with only a few tiny bedrooms and a single bathroom in the whole place. Cracked granite paving stones led from the driveway up to the modest front porch, its edges framed in with a wrought iron railing, black paint peeling, the metal beneath showing a dull gray. Above the porch perched two windows that let light into the second-story bedrooms. The windows had been added later, painstakingly cut from the solid frame with a handsaw, and their dimensions were just off enough from each other as to be noticeable. Slightly skewed. If the house was some squat, slouching beast, then those windows were its squinted eyes peering down at whomever dared to come disturb it.

No light showed through the curtains, so I didn't bother with the front door. Instead, I cut around the house to the right, through the long grass that grew wild in between the house and the detached garage. I rubbed dirt off a cracked window pane and peeked into the garage. Nearly empty, save for the accruement of forty-odd years in the construction game; bent ladders and sad shovels, dented trowels and rusted hammers, buckets of nails and screws and mismatched washers. A half pallet of concrete mix, dusty and cobwebbed and forgotten in one corner.

There had been a barn here once, my dad had told me, some ancient structure left over from the first family who had settled here. Above its hay door, the words *Ricker's Roost* had been painted around a horseshoe that had been nailed to the boards. The barn had collapsed long before I was born, and any remnant of it had sunk into the ground and disappeared like the bones of buffalo out on the prairie. The name, however, had stuck. *The Roost*; that's what we've always called this place. With the barn gone, the back yard behind the garage stretched from the fields to the east all the way to the muddy banks of the meandering Honey River to the west, with only the small green pond left in between to fill in the broad expanse.

The pond.

A body floated there, out toward the middle. Face down, greasy black hair spreading out like a rotted halo around pallid flesh, shirt and pants pulled tight, skin swollen beyond recognition. A fissure of blood and fragmented bone bloomed from the back of its skull, staining the water.

It had been waiting for me, just like I knew it would be.

A figure stood at the edge of the pond, his back to me. Slightly stooped and standing a little crooked, with a white t-shirt tucked into faded jeans held up by suspenders, all ending in a pair of green rubber boots. It looked more like a weathered scarecrow than a man. He must have heard me coming up through the yard, because when I was still a few dozen paces away the figure turned and squinted in my direction. His eyes crinkled behind his glasses amid a blossom of wrinkles.

"H-hey, Uncle Pete," I called, lifting a hand.

"Hey, yourself," he croaked. He wiped his hands on his shirt. A few thin whisps of gray hair fluttered in the wind around his stained trucker hat, and

I was reminded of just how long it'd been since I'd seen him. Years, now. Since the funeral. His mouth crooked into a boyish grin.

"How goes it, Marcus?"

"I'm doing alright, I guess."

I reached a hand out, and he took it with his own, pulled me into a surprisingly strong hug. We embraced for a moment, and I craned my neck to look past him, back to the water. The body was gone. Uncle Pete held me out in front of him with two hands on my shoulders, inspecting me like the contents of a time capsule he'd had buried for years and nearly forgot about. I couldn't help but grin.

"And how're you doin'?" I asked.

He shrugged. "Well, my arthritis feels like flames running up and down my wrists and my ankles, and my back has a few kinks that never seem to iron all the way out, and my bladder likes to remind me I gotta take a piss about two minutes after it happens." He gave a short, barking laugh. "Getting old's a bitch, Marcus. Don't ever do it." He glanced up at the dark clouds gathering in the distance. "If the rain stays away for us, I suppose I'll be just as happy as a pig in shit."

I laughed, and we embraced again. "It's good to see you, boy," Uncle Pete said, patting me on the back. "Lord knows it's been too long."

"Yeah, I know. I'm sorry…I keep meaning to get back this wa–" I started, but he waved me off.

"No need to speak it, Marcus. And no need to apologize. I know how quick the years go." As he said it, his eyes misted up a bit and drifted from me back to the clouds, then back down to the green water of the pond spreading out before us. He clapped me on the back. "I'm just glad you're here."

"Me too." I said it automatically, but not until the words left my mouth did I realize how true it was.

Uncle Pete ambled along the mossy bank of the pond, and I followed him. A couple ratty lawn chairs were set up in the grass a few yards off, right next to a large cooler. Closer to the water sat an old portable pump as big as the cooler, with dozens of loops of black hose coiled beside it. Uncle Pete bent down and grabbed one end of the hose, and when he straightened back up, he was wincing a bit. "Here," he said, holding out the hose, "run this end over there to the Honey if you would. Make sure it's well over the bank, but don't dip it in the water." I took the hose and started off toward the lazy little river out on the edge of the property. "Find a nice big rock and wedge it on top, so it don't go nowhere," Uncle Pete called out, and I waved my free hand.

Calling the Honey River a river was a bit generous. I suppose at some point in its life it had earned the name, but now, at the height of summer and with weeks since the last thunderstorm, it resembled little more than a creek, its clear water just a couple feet deep in the center. I hung the end of the hose over the bank, and with a few quick pulls, I tugged a good-sized rock out of the mud and set it on top. The water ran shallow, but it flowed swiftly, catching pieces of the few sunbeams that stabbed through the clouds, causing light to dance off the smooth, round rocks tucked away just below the water's surface. The Roost had never been my home, but there were times as a child when I got to spend days just like this one standing on this very same bank, making rafts out of tree bark and twigs and sending them off down the whirling waterways, watching them spin between the rocks and the minute eddies and the long-hanging grass, gliding above the minnows and the tadpoles until I could no longer see them. Part of me longed to be with them--sure they were destined for far-off oceans, some high seas adventure. I felt so free then, like some lost prince who had ventured too far from home and had to learn how to survive on their wits. It was the best kind of fantasy for a city kid.

My time spent at The Roost had been like that when I was young, some kind of fantasy life like the ones I loved to read about. The kids in the Narnia books, or Meg and Charles Murry in *A Wrinkle in Time*. The Boxcar Children. Kids in charge of their own lives, free to make decisions, to fight or run or hide or just explore. The Roost had been my Narnia, for a time; *my* side of the mountain. And I had free run of the place, from the fields to the forests beyond the river. Everywhere, in fact, but the pond. I was never allowed to go in the pond.

And the basement, I thought.

And then, *Marcus, I'm so scared. It's so dark down here.*

A chill spilled over me like ice water at the unbidden memory. I frowned. Had it been a memory, or had it been a dream? And who exactly had been scared? Who had said those words to me, so many years ago? I shook my head and pushed it away, pushed it all away. It was too nice of a day to think about that.

My days out here in Hilborn had been good ones, *that's* what I wanted to remember. Even if there weren't that many of them. "Want to go see your Uncle Pete?" my father would ask me, and then we'd be driving, and before the truck was even parked, I was off and running, heading straight for the river or the woods, barely even a hello or a goodbye to my dad and my uncle and my Aunt Laurie. I'd have mud stains on my knees and burrs on my shirt before I even caught my breath. Yeah, those were good days. The best, in fact. Until the last one. Until we stopped coming over to The Roost.

By the time I made my way back, Uncle Pete was already settled into one of the lawn chairs, an open Pabst in one hand, an unopened can in the other. He tossed me the beer and gestured toward the pump.

"She's all gassed up. Why don't ya see if that ol' sunuvabitch will turn over?"

It was an ancient thing, some relic that looked as if it had been pulled out of the bowels of some long-abandoned machine shop, rust spots showing through the dull black finish. Uncle Pete let loose with a burp as I examined the pump, and he wiped his mouth with the back of his hand. "Had it over to that Mennonite fella's shop a couple weeks ago…said it's running good now, but hell, I don't know. They make some damn good pies, you better believe, but I have a hard time trusting anybody that uses metal wheels on their tractors just to save themselves from gettin' too comfortable."

I laughed and sighed at the same time, my hands running over the back of the pump, searching for the pull-string. Same old Uncle Pete. "Yeah," I said, cocking an eye toward the tattered lawn chair sitting on crooked legs beside him. "You're a real expert when it comes to comfort." I found the handle of the string and pulled. The motor turned but stayed dead, so I braced my foot against the pump and pulled again. It kicked on with a sputtering roar. A puff of black smoke shot out from the exhaust, and then the engine evened out into a smooth, low rumble.

"Guess he knows what he's doin' after all," Uncle Pete said. I settled into the empty chair beside him and cracked my beer, and he held his out and tapped his can against mine. "Breakfast of Champions, huh? Cheers, boy."

"Cheers." I took a sip and felt the cold liquid rush through me. I probably should have eaten something before I came, knowing how Uncle Pete was. He had always been a bit of a drinker, but now, it seemed as if the habit had only gotten worse since Aunt Laurie passed away. Still, my college days weren't so far behind me that the taste of a beer at nine in the morning was a foreign thing. I took another long pull and felt myself start to relax. Tension in my neck and shoulders I hadn't even realized was there started to melt away, and I eased a little further into the chair, stretching my legs out toward the pond. I stole a quick glance over my shoulder back at the house.

Still there, of course. Still watching, another set of those crooked windows glancing out at us. A shudder ran through me, but I told myself it was just the cold beer getting settled.

"It's hard for you, ain't it?" Pete said, leaning back, his arms on the armrests. "Being here, I mean. Seeing it."

"No, I…no, it's ok."

"Bullshit. You look like you seen a ghost."

I smiled sheepishly, my mouth open and ready to say something to deflect the comment, but Pete cut me off.

"S'alright, you ain't gotta say nothin'. And you ain't gotta lie to me, I want that clear right from the get go." He took a pull off his can and smacked his lips. "Besides, it don't matter if you ain't seen a ghost or not." He smiled that crooked, boyish smile again.

"You will."

CHAPTER TWO

Uncle Pete sauntered back from the river. He took a long pull of his beer, then crushed the can with one hand. He tossed it beside the cooler with the other two empties. "She's flowing now," he said. He shielded his eyes with his hand and stared out over the pond. "Ain't too big, but I think it might take till dark to get her down to the bottom." He bent over the old pump and flipped a switch, and the motor guttered out and was silent. He grabbed another beer from the cooler and sat back down beside me. "That hose'll keep siphonin' the water out, and now we don't have to listen to the damn thing. Enough to make my head split."

Being with those who have known you since you were a child has a way of making you feel like you never grew up, like you're still that little kid they knew, no matter how many years you have under your belt. But death, the death of those close to you, it has a way of aging you, of changing you. It takes a piece of that innocence and it hardens it. Especially the death of a parent.

I nodded toward the pond. "You're not…you're not doing this 'cause of Dad, are you?"

Uncle Pete didn't look at me, but his face tightened all the same. I didn't think he was going to answer me, but then he sighed. "No, not 'cause ya dad, Marcus. Well, not *just* 'cause ya dad."

"Does the realtor want you to drain it?"

"Not particularly."

"I figured the pond would be a good selling point. People pay good money to get something like this in their backyard, don't they? I know it's not very deep, but you could still stock it with fish or something. They could probably throw some chemicals in here and clean it up enough to make it into a proper swimmin' hole."

Swimmin' hole. Jesus, not even back for an hour, and already the hillbilly patois was seeping back into me. I cringed a little, thinking of how hard it had been to rid myself of such things. *What the hell,* I thought, and took a sip of my Pabst. *When in Ohio.*

Uncle Pete snorted. "Nah, not this one, Marcus. You wouldn't wanna put so much as a pinky toe in that water. And anything you caught, you'd be better off just tossing it back in."

"Make you sick?"

"Oh yeah. And if you're lucky, that's all it'd do."

"I guess it's hard for me to believe you're really selling this place."

"Yeah, well," he said, with a wave of his hand. "Too much work for an old man like me." He turned and gave me a wink. "Not as young as I look."

I could tell he wasn't saying everything he wanted to, but I didn't push it. The sun was up, and although the mass of gray clouds above us started to thicken, the air stayed warm and it was turning out to be a pleasant day. Not too hot. A soft breeze was flitting through the stalks of corn like a warm ocean current rustling fronds in a kelp forest. The perfect day for sitting and talking and forgetting about the stress of life for a few hours. God, how long had it been since I was outside? Like *really* outside, not just rushing from apartment to car, from car to work, from work to car and back again. How long had it been since I spent time outside to just be outside. Months, for sure, maybe longer. Since Tera left, at least. I closed my eyes, felt the sun on my skin, listened to the birds and the wind and the distant splashing of the flowing water in the Honey River. I didn't want to ruin it.

When Uncle Pete had called me last week, I had let it go to voicemail. I *always* let it go to voicemail these days. But seeing his name pop up on my phone screen had filled me with an uneasiness I couldn't understand, some visceral feeling deep in my gut as if a hand had reached inside of me and started squeezing. Guilt, most likely, and a little shame. I'd never been good about keeping in touch; that was something that seemed to have been passed down from my father. But when I thought of Uncle Pete out here all alone, his wife ten years gone and his only brother following her just seven short years later, well, it made me feel like I needed to be there for him. I was the one who had lost a father, but he had lost someone, too. There was still a sense of responsibility there, some innately human need to comfort during a time of loss, to circle the wagons and pool our strength to get through the tough times together. I'd never reached out, though. Never called to see how he was holding up. I had Tera to help me, at least at first, and my job to distract me.

Yeah, Tera. I thought she'd be my forever. My wife. Mother of my children. And maybe…maybe she was supposed to be, if things had been different. But I fucked that up, just like so many other things in my life. Another box of regrets to lay at my dad's doorstep.

People always talk about the stages of grief, like when you experience it, there is a set path that you follow, clearly delineated steps that you walk up until you reach the end, and then—*poof*—it's over. You made it through to the other side. That's bullshit, of course. And maybe that's what people who have never experienced *real* grief think. Yeah, there are stages.

Denial. Anger. Bargaining. Depression. Acceptance.

But you don't go through each one and then on to the others. You go through them at the same time. The grief that I felt when Dad killed himself was an avalanche of emotions tumbling down on me from the moment I woke up to the moment I went to bed. It never stopped. I'd wake up sad, accept it by noon, be pissed off at him again by dinner, and by the time I drank myself to sleep, I wasn't even sure it had really happened. That maybe, if I grabbed my phone and dialed his old number, he would pick up and say, "Hey son, I was wonderin' when you was gonna give your old man a call."

And every day was different. Some mornings, I'd roll over, the hangover hitting me before I even opened my eyes, and I would reach for my phone in a panic, checking the messages to see if Dad had texted. Then would come the anger, or the sadness. The disconnecting from everything, from everyone. And Tera would be right there, trying to comfort me. But I was disconnecting from her, too.

You see, that's the other thing that you can't really understand about grief until you've gone through it yourself. Grief builds walls around you. It isolates. Even when you're grieving the same person, the same exact loss, grief makes it almost impossible to connect with someone else. It's a personal thing. We all deal with it differently. That was the main reason Uncle Pete and I hadn't talked in so long, I think. He was grieving a brother; I was grieving a father. Even though it was the same person, we weren't going through the same things.

Tera was a saint, and she tried to be there for me. But I didn't know how to let her do that. I hardly knew how to be there for myself.

Tera and I had met at work, her desk just a few cubicles down from mine. She had short, black hair, and a laugh that made my stomach feel all light and fluttery. I heard that laugh every so often, ringing out like a bell, breaking up the monotony of the office life, and I knew I had to talk to her. I made dumb, awkward small talk the first few times I saw her. Stupid things, trying to get to hear that laugh in person. To be the cause of it for once. Finally, I think she took pity on me, told me if I ever wanted to have a real conversation, then maybe I could take her out somewhere so we could talk. Somewhere less soul-crushing than the office environment. We had our first date a week later, and a month after that, she moved into my apartment. Things were great, those first four years. Until Dad killed himself. And then the grief came to live with us, and I never heard her laugh again.

"You have to let me in, Marcus," she told me one Saturday morning.

I'd passed out on the couch, like I'd been doing lately. Not because I didn't enjoy sleeping beside her, but because I'd come to think of my grief as some sort of communicable disease. I didn't want to infect her. She was kneeling beside me, running the back of her hand down my cheek. When I opened my eyes, I saw that her own eyes were wet and dazzling.

"I want to help you get through this. But I can't do that if you keep shutting me out."

"I'm not shutting you out," I said, knowing I was.

"You are, though. And it hurts me. You know it's hurting me too, right? Watching you do this to yourself."

"I can't…I can't worry about someone else's pain right now."

"But what about *your* pain? You can't keep running from it. It's not just going to go away some day. You have to…you have to fight for it. You have to fight for yourself. For us."

"I've never been a fighter." I gave her a weak smile. She didn't return it. I tried again. "Listen, I just…I don't want to talk about it right now, ok? I just…I can't."

"Can't? Or won't?"

"What's the difference?"

A single tear fell from her eye and ran down her cheek. I didn't feel anything.

"Yeah," she said, nodding. "What's the difference?"

She packed her stuff up that night. She was gone the next morning, off to her mom's, I think. I never asked. I never called. I never begged her to stay, either. She gave me a kiss on my cheek when she left, her eyes red from crying. Still, I felt nothing.

The apartment sat quiet and empty, and so did I.

And although that empty feeling my father had left when he killed himself was still there inside of me like a black whirlpool of despair wanting nothing more than to pull my hope and my happiness down with it, I had found a way to keep it locked up deep inside of me—to strangle it until it would shut the fuck up and leave me alone for a while. I had to, you know, to survive. Or else it would have dragged me under its dark waters. So, when Uncle Pete had called me, I felt that dark whirlpool rush a little faster, its ears perking up like a prisoner who hears the rattle of keys when the jailer starts getting close to his cell. I turned my cell phone face down on my desk so I didn't have to look at it, told myself I'd call him later, a part of me knowing I'd actually just keep turning the phone over again and again rather than have to risk a walk by that prison cell. It'd be uncomfortable, and it would eat at me over time, but it was safer this way. Better.

I don't know why I called him back, not even now. It was like some stranger got inside me, started pulling levers I had long abandoned, because before I could change my mind, I was turning my phone back over and dialing his number, hands shaking and breath coming quick.

He had picked up on the first ring. "Marcus," he said. "You got time this weekend to come help an old man?"

"Sure, Uncle Pete," I breathed out. "What do you need help with?"

"Burying a few bodies." The silence stretched out a bit, then he laughed.

"Nah, nothin' quite so sinister. But maybe just as dirty. Gotta get The Roost ready for market, and I could use an extra set of hands around here." He hesitated. "Mostly, I could use the company, truth be told."

I looked around my studio apartment, at the pizza boxes and beer cans stacked up precariously beside the trashcan like a game of Jenga in the final round, at the piles of clothes on the empty bed, at the empty couch. "I'll be there," I told him. "Yeah, I'll head that way as soon as I get a cup of coffee in me. I think I could use the company, too." I regretted making the call as soon as I hung up. The stranger—the one who'd made me pick up the phone in the first place—vanished, and I was alone again.

"You know, ya daddy weren't the first person to die in that water."

I looked up with a start. I'd been staring out toward the Honey, toward the woods on its far bank. I'd nearly forgotten what we'd been talking about. I cleared my throat.

"What do you mean?"

He leaned forward, his elbows perched on his knees, his beer held down between his legs.

"What I mean is your daddy weren't the first body to be pulled out of there, son." He cocked an eye over toward me. "I don't mean to be bringing him up. My mouth is old and the brakes got worn off a couple decades ago, and sometimes it just runs and runs and it don't stop until I can jam my foot all the way inside of it."

"It's alright, really. I…I don't talk about him much, that's all." I shrugged. "Maybe I need to."

Uncle Pete nodded at that, turned his head back out toward the green water.

"Somebody else died here?" I asked. "In the pond?"

"More than one." He seemed to sink into his chair a bit, a tire with a slow leak. "Christ, I never thought I'd talk about this again. Swore I wouldn't, in fact. But in a few weeks, this place won't be mine no more, won't be the *family's*, and I s'pose there are a few burdens I wouldn't mind shrugging off my shoulders before that time comes." He cocked an eye at me. "That is, if you don't mind slogging through some old muck with me."

"I don't mind," I said. "But shouldn't we be, I don't know, moving boxes or something? Packing stuff up?"

"Nah, there's plenty of time for that." He waved his hand. "All the time for that. I'd rather set here a spell and catch up with my favorite nephew."

I shrugged. "I'd be happy to just sit here all day and drink if that's what you want to do. Spill it, Uncle Pete. I want to hear all the dirty family secrets."

Uncle Pete almost smiled. Almost. He took a deep breath.

"Now, most people will say that the best place to start a story is at the beginning. But I don't think I can do that. Not *this* story. I gotta come at it sideways…if I try to go rushing in headlong, I might lose my nerve. Gotta ease into it." He breathed out heavy a couple times as if psyching himself up, the way I imagine a cliff diver might before making the plunge.

"You need a refill?" he asked.

"Still got a few sips left."

He reached into the cooler, grabbed another white can, and handed it to me along with a sandwich wrapped in deli paper. He grabbed another beer for himself, too.

"Take this one anyway," he said. "Believe me, Marcus. You're going to need it."

CHAPTER THREE

"Nearly every person who ever lived at The Roost has died here."

A grim sort of determination crossed Uncle Pete's face. Hard lines were etched into the skin around his eyes and his mouth as if chiseled into granite. He gazed out toward the pond, but I could tell he wasn't seeing it. He stared through it, through a fog, back through the tangled webs of years gone by.

"I don't mean to *just* say that people have died here, neither. My great-grandpa James—*your* great-great-grandpa, the one your dad was named after—he built that house back there in the spring and summer of 1904. And when a place holds that much history, it'd be on the strange side if people *hadn't* died on the property. People lived a lot closer to death back in them days, Marcus. Hell, it was custom to hold the funeral right inside your home, the body right up on the kitchen table for all the friends and neighbors to come pay their respects, nothing but a sheet separating ya dear Uncle Ernest from where you had ya Sunday dinner. No, I don't mean that people have just died here. They died *wrong* here.

"My father—your Grandpa Gabe, God rest his soul—you never got to meet him. He was dead and in the ground a handful of years before you came into this world. Ya daddy ever tell you what happened to him? What happened out here?"

I finished chewing a bite of ham and cheese and swallowed, cleared my throat. "You know how Dad was. He didn't talk about when he was a kid too much—too *often*. About your guy's childhood. He said…he said Grandpa Gabe was a hard man to be around. He said you and him were up before sunrise every day, rain or shine. That you had to feed the cows and the chickens and the goat, get the milk and the eggs inside the house before you could get ready for school or else you'd be going to school with welts on your asses." Pete chuckled at that, but he did it almost grudgingly. "But no," I continued, "he never talked about the later years. When Grandpa died, I mean."

"And he wouldn't have. They wasn't really close after…after James moved away, you know. Not that Daddy blamed him much, but still. The old man took it hard. 'Course it don't matter much whether ya dad said anything about ya grandpa, how he died, I mean. No way to stop the people in town from talkin'. Hard to keep something like that under wraps, especially out here where everyone knows each other's business. I figured you would've heard a whisper or two when you came to visit, but you was young then. You was spared the worst of it by not having to grow up out here. Jim shielded you that much, at least.

"It was March of 1989, and goddam if that winter before it wasn't a real bastard." Pete sat forward and half turned in his chair, the worn strapping creaking. He gazed back toward the house. "The snow came down that year something biblical. Drifts as high as that window there in the garage. Me and Laurie were living over in Mansfield back then. She was working at Mansfield General as an ER nurse, and she was making good money, too, you better believe. It weren't much of a city, far as those things go, no Cleveland or Columbus or Cincinnati or what have you, but it was just big enough and just crowded enough for a country bumpkin like me to feel a little out of sorts. And though me and Dad weren't on the best of terms, I missed The Roost something awful. Before the snow got real bad, I used to come back here on the weekends to help around the place. Daddy was retired, but he still had a yard full of animals to take care of. Mostly I'd come and see that they were tended to. Dad never said thank you—never gave so much as a head nod, to be honest—but I never did it for him. Didn't even see him most days. It kept me grounded, you understand? Got me out of the city for a bit. Kept me sane. But that winter of '88 was like nothing I'd ever seen." He leaned forward and sighed, and it was like a rockslide tumbling down a small mountain. His voice grew thick. "It kept me away. The roads weren't clear from November to March, not that I couldn't have got through them with my pickup, but it was just as good an excuse as any to not come out here. Not that Daddy was begging me or nothing. But, you know, I always figured if there was some kind of trouble...I don't know, maybe he was running low on food, or maybe that old furnace in the basement conked out...I always figured he would get a hold of me. So when I didn't hear a word from him all winter, well, I didn't think nothin' of it." He raised his hands out in front of him, beer in one, the other palm up as if in supplication. "I didn't know.

"It was the second week of March when I got the call. I had a big job set up in Wooster, a new build I'd won a bid for. *Big* house...one of them split-level jobs that were popular back then. Castle Construction was staying afloat through a dozen or so contracts, but they'd all been piecemeal; pour a foundation here, build a garage there. Re-shingle a roof, stuff like that. We were getting a good reputation, but this was a big one for us. A straight ticket to the next level, yessir. I'd hired on a half-dozen fellas or so. All this is just to say that when the snow finally started to melt, Dad and The Roost might as well have been a million miles away from my mind. So, when Sheriff Brown called me, it took a long while for me to register what he was sayin'.

"*Come home, Pete*, he said. *Come home just as fast as you can.* And when I asked him what was shaking, all he would say is, *It's your daddy*. Well, I hauled ass getting back here, nearly ditching my pickup a few times on the way. By the time I made the drive, there were already a handful of police cruisers in the front yard. Mostly from the Sheriff's Department, but there was a statie, too. Ambulance and a firetruck to boot, but there weren't no smoke. A couple of officers tried to stop me when I got out of the truck, but I pushed them out of my way. The house was empty. I could hear voices comin' from back here, back toward the pond. Sherrif Brown caught sight of me when I rounded the corner. He tried to cut me off, too—*Pete, wait. Pete, hold on. Pete, no.* But I don't think I even heard him. Cold, that's what I remember, not what the Sheriff was saying. Wind so goddam cold it'd freeze the words before they even got out your mouth. And the blood. I remember the blood.

"They'd found Pop out there, out in the middle of the water. The pond was frozen then, of course, and he'd been slumped down on top the ice. Wasn't wearin' shoes or a hat or nothin'. Just a pair of long johns. His hands…his hands was…mangled. Fingers peeled back all the way to the bone. Christ, it was awful. There was a broken wood chisel beside him, the blade nicked, the wood handle cracked and separated. He'd been digging, digging. Stabbing and chipping away until the handle split. Then he'd started clawing with his fingers. The cold must have numbed him something good, cause the paramedics told me later that it weren't humanly possible to keep going on, the way he was injured. The bones of his fingers were all sticking through the ripped skin, but that wasn't the worst of it. The bones themselves were worn down. Shaved clean down past the first knuckle, like, like a power sander had got to them."

My stomach twisted. I could feel the ham and cheese and bread boiling in my stomach, threatening to come back up. Uncle Pete wasn't looking too good himself. His Pabst was shaking in his hand. I knew without him having to tell me that this wasn't something he'd ever talked about. Pieces of it, maybe, but not the whole thing. Not the details.

"God," he spit out. "God, it's just so fucking awful, pardon my French."

"What…what was he even doing out there? Why…why was he out on the ice?"

"Who knows? Hypothermia was one thing…there were signs of frostbite on his toes and on the edge of his nose. You know, that stuff don't happen once a body stops breathing. He must have been out there for hours. Got a bit of the snow-madness, I think. But…but that ain't everything. That was the worst of it, but that ain't all. There was the animals, too."

"The animals?"

"Yep, the chickens, the handful of cows. Fuck, even the goat, Marcus. Poor bastard." Pete sighed. "He killed them."

"Killed them?"

Pete nodded. "Every last one of them. When I came back here, they'd already taken Pop away under a sheet. I…I could still see the ring of blood and cracked ice where they'd found him. But the animals were still out there. All of them. Their bodies littered the ice like someone's sick idea of lawn decorations. The cows, they must have been led there, one by one. There were five of them, and though the ice was thawing a bit, I could still see where they lay, slumped together in a semi-circle near where they'd found Pop. Each one had been shot in the head. Pop had an old .45 he used to keep around for the coyotes, and each one of them heifers had a hole right through their skull. There were the chickens, too, eight or ten of them, their necks broken, bodies all tossed about willy-nilly. No real rhyme or reason to it. But the goat…the goat was different. Daddy'd had that old goat for fifteen years or so. Closest thing to a pet he'd ever made out of a farm animal. The goat had been stabbed to death…that damn wood chisel, no doubt. Stabbed a dozen times and laid down on its stomach right next to Pop, its legs broken and splayed out. Looked kind of like one of them bear rugs, but if the bear had never been gutted or deboned or whatever. Daddy had cut its throat, too, and its blood had seeped into the cracks that was cut into the ice. There was hardly a clean speck of snow or ice. It was just red, Marcus, from one end to the other. Nothing but red."

Uncle Pete was looking out over the pond, his eyes unfocused, his beer momentarily forgotten in his hand. I stared at the pond, too, trying to picture what it must have looked like on that cold day in March. I caught glimpses in my mind of that snow-covered ice painted red, of the frozen bodies strewn across it. I blinked, and then the snow was gone, and I saw the body again. Face-down, floating in the still green water while the crickets chirped in the long grass along the bank. The gun somewhere below him, lying in the muck and mud at the bottom of the pond. Christ. Pete had found him, too—found Dad out there. For the first time that morning I felt the weight of grief crashing against the walls I'd put up inside myself, felt those walls shake at the seams. Mortar cracking, bolts shimmying loose. I wiped the corner of my eye with the back of my hand and coughed.

Uncle Pete looked over. He tried another one of those crooked smiles, but it didn't fit right on his face.

"Heavy stuff, huh, kid?"

"Yeah," I breathed out.

"Jim never told you none of that?"

"No. I never really asked him about it either…I could tell it wasn't something he wanted to talk about. I just…I knew Grandpa died out here, died at The Roost. I just figured he'd had a heart attack or something. I don't know what I thought."

"He wasn't a bad man, you know. Grandpa Gabe, I mean. He was hard on us growing up. Harder than he had to be, maybe. But he didn't beat us unless we deserved it. Didn't treat the animals unkindly. He wasn't cruel. What happened here at the end, it just…that weren't my daddy. I just want you to know that, Marcus. That was something else." He shook his head softly, Peter denying Christ for the third, final time. "It's been years now, but I still can't wrap my head around it. Still can't get that blood out my mind. I guess…you'd think it'd get easier the older you get, forgettin' them things you don't want to think about. Not that, though. Some kinds of bad just don't worsh off."

CHAPTER FOUR

My dad had never told me what happened to Grandpa Gabe, but now that I knew the whole story, I couldn't hold it against him. A part of me *wanted* to hold it against him, though, wanted to be mad at that chickenshit asshole again, just to throw another stick on the fire of my rage. But, when would have been a good time for a story like that? At my graduation party? At Christmas dinner? I never knew what happened, but I always knew *something* had happened. I never heard him talking about it, never heard a whispered conversation on the phone or behind closed doors when we would visit Uncle Pete and Aunt Laurie. No, I knew something had happened because of what they *didn't* say. Kids can tell stuff like that. They learn just as much about life from what they're allowed to do as what they're not. They know that the movies they aren't allowed to watch, the music they aren't allowed to listen to, the friends they're not supposed to hang around with…*those* are the things that will teach them the most, the things they'll never learn from their parents. Those are the things they *want* the most. The surest way for a kid to find out something is for his parents to tell him he isn't allowed to know it. Dad hardly ever brought up Grandpa at all, and when he did, it was mostly small anecdotes, little offhand remarks thrown out like random slashes of a very small paintbrush, just enough to add a little color, never enough to complete a full picture. And that was more than enough for a young me to want to seek him out, to learn everything I could. I peppered him with questions whenever he seemed to be in a good mood, whenever he'd had more than a couple drinks after dinner, but still, I knew so little about my grandpa.

I knew that Grandpa Gabe liked horses, that *his* dad had even had a couple around The Roost back when Grandpa was a boy. I knew he loved animals, had even made Dad and Uncle Pete go to bed hungry one night when they had forgotten to feed the cows. I knew he liked Hank Williams, and playing horseshoes, and he smoked unfiltered cigarettes he would roll himself. But that was it. Hearing Pete tell his story, telling such a horrific tale about my own flesh and blood, it left me feeling a bit numb, a bit distanced from myself. Like it hadn't actually happened to someone in our family, but was just a story in a book, some stranger's tale. It was driving down a highway you'd been down a thousand times before, only to wind up smack dab in a town that had never been there before, one that wasn't on any map you'd ever seen. The Roost didn't feel quite so familiar anymore.

Uncle Pete got up and stretched, his wrinkled hands planted in the small of his back. I wanted to get up, too, but I wasn't sure if my legs would hold me just then. I watched him wander over to where the hose snaked into the green water, staggering like a landlubber trying to get their sea legs. Could have been the beer, but I knew it was more than that. Satisfied with the hose, he stood there on the edge of the water. He took great care that his feet didn't go beyond the grass. The water in the pond had dropped noticeably since we'd been sitting here. Just a few inches, but it was moving. He mumbled something, just a few words, but it was so low the wind took them from his mouth before I could hear them. He nodded once, then walked back and eased himself into the chair beside me. He pulled a rumpled pack of Camels out of his shirt pocket and shook one out. He lit it and held the smoke in for a few seconds. He coughed twice, hard, and smoke bloomed out of him.

"You alright over there?"

He hacked a few more times, waving me off with a hand.

"Shoulda quit these damn things years ago," he said, once the coughing fit passed. "Better yet, I never shoulda started in the first place." He took another drag, and this time it went down easy. He cocked his head at me and lifted the pack partially out of his pocket again, eyebrows raised. "No thanks," I said, and he nodded, settling back into his chair.

"How long do you think it will take to empty it out?" I said. I checked the time on my phone. 11:30. I couldn't help but notice there weren't any notifications. There hardly ever were these days. It seemed people could only send so many unanswered messages before they gave up. That was fine. I tucked my phone back into my pocket and took in the yard and the pond and the trees in the distance. Somewhere above the mass of gray clouds, the sun drew closer to its zenith, though it was hard to tell from where we sat. Uncle Pete glanced at me, had noticed me putting my phone away.

"You getting antsy? You got a hot date tonight or somethin'?"

I thought of Tera, then pushed her away, forced out a laugh. "No, not tonight. I got absolutely nothing going on. I'm all yours, Uncle Pete."

"C'mon, now, don't be lyin' to an old man. Don't got someone to be with? What about work? No one there catchin' ya fancy?"

I shook my head. "No, I've been working there too long…seeing the same people every day. Nobody really does it for me."

"Ahh, bullshit!" Uncle Pete said, waving a hand. "That ain't how it works. You never heard the story of the two monkeys?" I shook my head.

"Well, you ever get stuck on an island with two monkeys, sooner or later, one of them monkeys gonna start lookin' a whole lot prettier than the other. Same goes for folks you work with."

He cackled out a bray of laughter, and I couldn't help myself but to join in.

"Nah, I'm just yankin' your chain," he said. "But I wouldn't blame you none if you got other things on ya mind. This here's 'bout as exciting as watchin' paint dry, ain't it?"

"Ah, it's not that bad. We have these comfy chairs and a cooler full of beer. Plus, this nice beachfront view," I said with a laugh. "We're basically just going fishing without any poles."

Uncle Pete burst into another hacking, coughing laugh. "That's right, Marcus," he said between coughs. "That's just about right." He reached over and slapped me on the back, held my shoulder for a moment in his hand.

There was something about the way he looked at me that reminded me of my dad. Something familiar in the way his eyes seemed to sparkle. I felt a pressure building behind my eyes, so I smiled, and said, "You know, I used to love this place when I was a kid."

Uncle Pete smiled and sat back. "Well, we used to love having you here, too, kiddo. Laurie and me, we never had kids ourselves, you know. No cousins for you. It did her a lot of good to have you running around out here, even when you was getting into trouble."

There must have been something showing on my face, because Uncle Pete snorted. "Yeah, I'm talking about you, Marcus Allen Castle. You was always polite, don't get me wrong, but every kid's got a bit of a wild animal inside of 'em, and you wasn't no different. All the times your aunt had to mop up muddy footprints on her clean linoleum..." He whistled. "But Laurie never once did hold it against ya. Now me, on the other hand, if I ever forgot to take my work boots off at the door, I never heard the end of it." He was silent for a moment, and when I stole a glance his way, I swore I saw the twinkle of wetness at the corner of his eyes. He didn't look sad, though, at least not all the way.

"She was a sweet woman," I ventured.

"That she was. She put up with my ass for forty years, through rain or shine, hell and heartbreak. Damn if I don't miss her every day."

"I'm sorry."

"Ah, don't be. No fool worse than an old fool." He took a sip from his freshly opened can. "Anyway, I didn't drag you out here to bring up all these old, painful memories. I promise I didn't, regardless of how it's turning out."

"You did say you needed help burying some bodies, though."

"Yeah, and I suppose I do. But it seems to me we ain't burying any bodies; the bodies 'round here, they've been buried a long time. We're just sitting here digging 'em right back up."

"At least you ain't—at least you're not out here digging them up alone."

"True. But there's still more buried around here yet."

He looked old then, older than I'd ever seen him. Something in the way the gray, flat light seemed to coat his face, filling in the wrinkles around his eyes and his mouth, making them seem as deep as the furrows in a freshly plowed field. "You don't have to keep going," I said, "you know, if you don't want to."

"That's the bitch of it though. I *do* have to. I don't want to, but I do. You hold onto these things for so long, they start hollowing you out. They get in your blood like poison and just eat atcha until there ain't nothin left." He stared at his beer, running a calloused thumb around and around the rim. "There ain't nobody left but you and me, Marcus. Once we're gone, it's all over. All of this will be forgotten. Maybe it's better that way. But I don't wanna go in the ground with these things still inside me.

"I guess it's time you heard about Natalie. And Michael."

CHAPTER FIVE

"They used to say that someone born under a full moon was touched by the devil. Did you know that? Lunacy, ya know; that didn't always just mean crazy. 'Course, we know that's horseshit now, but back when Natalie was just a baby, it was still close enough to them old days that some of those old wives' tales was still scripture. Especially out here in God's country. Don't walk under a ladder, don't cross a black cat…if you spill the salt, throw some over your shoulder. You get the picture. Well, Natalie was born in the Autumn of 1933, right in the heart of the Depression, and under the biggest harvest moon folks around here had seen in years. She was your great-aunt, sister to my daddy and their older brother William. And she was cursed, just like all of us.

"She was the only Castle to ever been born right here at The Roost, right in the living room. Her momma, Lenore, she'd already give birth to two boys, but by the time Natalie come, her body about done gave up on her. She'd turned thin and sickly, and the pregnancy was a tough one. Natalie was s'posed to be a winter baby, but she came early. 'Bout a month early, matta fact. Damn near killed her *and* Lenore, but they survived. God help 'em, they survived.

"According to my daddy, the family knew Aunt Natalie was different by the time she was four or so. She was a late bloomer in a lot of ways. She didn't walk—even *try* to walk—until she was three, until one day she just stood up and started strutting around the house. Same goes for talkin', too. They thought maybe she was deaf or somethin' like that. Didn't cry like a normal kid, didn't do none of that goo-goo ga-ga bullshit. In fact, she didn't say a peep until right around her fourth birthday. And when she did start talkin', it weren't no baby talk. It was full sentences, Marcus. And she used big words. Grownup words. My daddy said they was out playing in the back yard one day, and little Natalie looked up at him, and she said, 'I'd like to go back inside the house now, Gabriel.' Just like that—damn near knocked Daddy out." Pete shook his head at the wonder of it, like he could see it happening right in front of us. I almost could, too. He took off his hat, exposing his freckled, balding pate, and wiped his brow, then he continued.

"Now, little kids like to babble; seems like as soon as they figure out how to work their voicebox, they pull that switch and just leave the damn thing runnin' unless someone shuts 'em up. Natalie was a babbler, but it didn't seem to the rest of the family that she was ever talkin' just to talk, wasn't stringin' words together just to hear herself speak. It was as if she was talkin' to somebody. Having a conversation. She'd say a full sentence, maybe ask a question, then she'd pause, like she was waiting for someone to answer her. Like she was listenin'. But no one was ever around. A couple times Daddy caught her talkin', and he asked her who she was talking to, but she would just shake her head and not say nothin'. And when Daddy would walk away, he'd hear her start up again, only her voice would be lower, hushed up, like she didn't want Daddy to hear what she was sayin'. This went on for a few years, and the family just sort of got used to it, the way you do when you have to deal with something odd day in and day out. They never said nothin', didn't think twice about it. But they should have."

Uncle Pete leaned forward and propped his elbows on his legs, his hands clasped together around his beer. He closed his eyes for a couple of seconds, then opened them back up.

"Natalie tried to kill her momma when she was six."

"What the fu–"

"There's just no way to sugarcoat it, Marcus. Natalie tried to kill her momma. Grandma Lenore was at the top of the stairs that lead down into the basement. You know, right next to the pantry in the kitchen?"

He looked to me, and that voice came to me again, the one I'd thought of earlier over by the Honey.

Marcus, I'm so scared. It's so dark down here.

It had been a girl's voice, I remembered now. I put my hands in my lap to try and stop them from shaking. All I could do was nod to Uncle Pete.

Yes, I remembered the door to the basement stairs. I remembered them very well.

Uncle Pete didn't seem to notice my discomfort. He nodded, saying, "Well, Lenore was right there, armful of preserves she'd just got done canning, getting ready to take 'em down and put 'em up on the shelves. Natalie came up behind her and shoved her. Shoved her *hard*. She was a little thing, skinny like all them Depression kids, but Grandma Lenore's arms were full and she couldn't stop herself. She fell down those stairs, and those glass jars of peppers and pickles fell right down alongside her. She landed on the concrete floor in a pile of busted glass. Grandpa Howard had been right outside the back door and came runnin' in when he heard the commotion, and he found Natalie just standing at the top of the stairs, gazing down into that darkness. Her own momma was down there, just screaming and screaming, and there was little Natalie, just watchin' her scream.

"Grandpa Howard shoved Natalie outta the way and ran down to Grandma. She was busted up pretty badly, I guess…she'd broke an ankle during the fall, and sprained her wrist. Her face had smacked against the concrete floor, and her nose was all busted up. There was blood and juice and jam all over her from all the broken jars, and she had glass sticking out from her arms and legs and cheeks like it was growing out her skin. Daddy and his older brother Michael had been playing upstairs and had rushed down by then. Daddy said Natalie wasn't just standing there by the time they got to her. She was talkin' to herself, the way she did. *I'm sorry, I'm sorry,* she was whispering. Over and over. *I'm sorry.*" Pete shook his head. "And then, when Daddy got closer, before Natalie knew he was there, he heard her say, *Next time, I promise, Mr. Trench. I'm sorry.*"

I shuddered, a coolness spreading over me like river water during a spring thaw. I knew those stairs, had been in that kitchen with the door to the basement wide open a hundred times. They were steep. And I knew the darkness that waited at the bottom. Like I said, The Roost had been updated over the years, modernized here and there, but it was an *old* house. And while the skin of the place had been cleaned up and polished, new furniture and new appliances and a fresh coat of paint every so often, the bones of the place are still the same as they were when it was built. Those stairs should have been torn out fifty years ago. The steps weren't wide enough, for one thing, and the space between each step was too high. They were a death trap; just walking down them could be perilous. I couldn't imagine being *shoved* down them. It was a wonder my Great-Grandma Lenore survived the fall. I was so caught up in the horror of it, it took a while for me to process the last few words Uncle Pete had said. And when I did, I looked up at him sharply. He was looking at me, as if waiting for it to click.

"Mr. Trench?" I said, my mouth suddenly dry. "Who was Mr. Trench?"

"I was wonderin' if you caught that. Mr. Trench was…well, that was who Natalie had been talkin' to all them years, apparently. Her…

imaginary friend."

He's lying, someone whispered in my ear. So close, I felt their breath on the back of my neck. It smelled of rot. I gripped the chair, whipped my head around. But there was no one there. No one, except for the house.

I frowned, but Uncle Pete just laughed. It was a harsh, brittle sound. Like snapping bones, or broken glass tumbling across a concrete floor.

"Gettin' spooked, huh?" He laughed again. "You have to remember when all this happened. It was a hard time, and it was a hard time all over. Whole country was goin' to Hell. Farmland had been gutted, thousands of families removed from their homesteads, moving in masses out to the edges of the country, trying to find work and food. Just trying to survive. We were sheltered a little here…Ohio didn't get nearly as bad as say Kansas or Oklahoma. But that don't mean it was no spring picnic. And yeah, they had head doctors then, too. But working the land requires sacrifice. It takes your blood and your sweat and it takes all your time. Every decision is a hard decision when you're just a week or two of bad luck away from losing everything. All this is to say, that by then the family knew that whatever was wrong with Natalie was more than just a…whaddyacallit…a *phase* or somethin'. But just like death, just like everything, they kept it close. Kept it to themselves. They figured they could just work through it, the way they worked through all the hard times. They was wrong.

"Three years later, just a few weeks after Natalie's ninth birthday, almost all of them was dead. Grandma Lenore, Natalie, Michael…all but my daddy and Grandpa Howard. And Grandpa Howard was gone not too long after that. A house full of people, then," and Pete snapped his fingers. "Then, nothing."

Uncle Pete stood up then, so quick it startled me. He rubbed at the small of his back, his face turned up to the clouds. Across the pond, a bit more of the moss-covered bottom showed. The water level had dropped a few more inches, and the exposed ground shined a startling gray between the clumps of leaves and mulch and decaying algae stuck to the bottom, like a bit of bone showing through rotting flesh. It made me uneasy looking at it, so I turned back to Uncle Pete instead. Somehow, he was almost worse.

He was crying. Not just a glimmer of wetness at the corner of his eyes this time, but full-on streams of tears coating his cheeks. He pulled a handkerchief from his shirt pocket and wiped at his face.

"You alright, Uncle Pete?" Dumb thing to say, of course. Who the hell is alright when they're crying? But it was something you said when there was nothing else to say. Like "I'm sorry."

I'm sorry, Mr. Trench, I thought, and I felt my skin prickle.

"Yeah, I'm okay," Uncle Pete said. He blew his nose in the hanky, then stuffed it back into his shirt pocket. "Like I said, no fool like an old fool."

He settled back into his chair, and his face settled with him, the creases at the corners of his eyes and mouth smoothing what little they could. He was quiet for a moment, but I didn't push him.

"You know," he said, once he came back to himself. "I never met any of these folks. They're kin, through and through, but other than my daddy, they was all gone long before I was born. I 'spose that's what really gets to me. It ain't what happened to them, not exactly, anyway. It's what could have been, you know? It's what I lost. Me and Jim could have had an aunt and an uncle. We could have grown up with grandparents that doted on us and loved us, made us cookies and gave us Christmas presents, taught us about life and what their lives were like when they was kids. I think…I think maybe Daddy would've been nicer, too. If he didn't…if he didn't go through what he went through. But also, if his parents were around, you know, to guide him a bit. I think it would have smoothed some of the edges off him."

There was something to that. Dad was always good to me. It could have been because he had me so late in his life, but I couldn't help but wonder what might have been. By the time I was born, he was a middle-aged man, and he had drank and fought and strangled all his demons away.

The body in the water flashed in and out of my mind.

Nearly all his demons.

Uncle Pete straightened in his seat. "I'm putting the cart before the horse, I realize that, but all this history's been stirring something up inside of me, and I needed to get a bit of it out if I was gonna finish this damn thing. And that's what I aim to do, right here before you and God and everything else. I'm gonna finish it." He took his hanky out one more time and dabbed at his face.

"So, three years later, they was all dead. Snuffed out. Hard to say exactly how it all started, with so much time between now and then, but I know what my daddy told me, and what his daddy told him. At the center of all that death, at the heart of all that evil, was this very pond.

"Even back then, this pond was off limits to all the kids. It weren't an age thing; Michael was the oldest, and even he wasn't to go near it. No swimming, of course, and no fishing. They weren't even allowed to use the water for the animals. You see that pipe over there?" Pete asked me. He pointed off across the pond, over to where a metal pipe stuck up from the ground, a red-handled spigot stuck on its end. "That there is what they used for the animals. Grandpa Howard's dad James, he run the pipe himself, straight from the Honey. That's what he used to fill the damn thing in the first place, but later on, that's all he would give to the animals. Guess they thought it was cleaner. This pond…well, shit, there was something wrong with it. Hardly a day went by when they wouldn't find some sort of dead animal floating in the water here. Groundhogs, racoons, opossums. Squirrels and chipmunks. Birds, too, ducks and geese and such. I mean, take a look, Marcus. The water's getting lower now, almost low enough to see the bottom in the shallow parts. You see any fish in there? You see any frogs?"

I glanced at the water again. Just those odd graying clumps between the masses of mud and algae. No fish. No frogs.

"No, sir," I said.

"And you won't, not live ones, at least. It's tainted. Tainted, cursed, whatever word you wanna call it. It weren't meant for living things. But Natalie…little Natalie had it set in her head that she had to get in that water. She cried for it. *Begged* for it. And when her mama said no, she'd scream for it. Caught her right here a half-dozen times, her toes or ankles dipping in the water. More than once, Grandpa Howard set it on her backside with this stripped piece of hickory he kept by the back door. His whipping switch, he called it. He'd lay into her something good, get her so she couldn't sit down for a week or two without crying from the bruises and the welts. But it never stopped her. And, 'course, they couldn't keep an eye on her *all* the time.

"She got in there anyway. Not just her toes or her feet, but *all* the way in. Only once, but once was enough. Little Natalie had gotten worse in the years since she pushed Lenore down the basement steps. She never talked to nobody, 'cept for herself, and she did that almost constantly. Out loud, but lots of times she'd just be sittin' there, starin' at the wall, lips movin' but no sound comin' out. Like watchin' the TV on mute. And the outbursts, oh Lord…be just right as rain one minute, the next, she's howlin' and screamin'. She grabbed her fork one night at dinner and jumped at Grandpa Howard. Stabbed that sunuvabitch right into his arm. Eight or ten stitches and it never did heal right. Had that scar till the day he died. He damn near killed her for that. There were other times, too, other…*incidents*. It was like something in her little girl's brain had gone sour. There was a violence in her that ought not to be in a child.

"They'd taken to locking her in her bedroom at night, so as they could keep an eye on her. Keep her safe. Most of the harm she'd done had been done to others, never to herself, you understand, so Grandma and Grandpa thought they was doing right by keeping her up there. But they underestimated the will of the child. The persistence of the demon that was inside of her."

Uncle Pete half turned in his chair and pointed up to the house, to the crooked second story window on the left.

"That window right there was where her bedroom was. Whaddya reckon that is, 'bout sixteen feet or so?" He turned back and faced the pond. He didn't once look at me. "Well, she jumped from that window in the middle of the night. Didn't even open the window, just broke right through the single-pane glass. It was a full moon, and the way Daddy told it to me, the yard must have been lit up like a Christmas tree, everything glowing in the pale light. The fall broke her left ankle—just like she'd done to her Momma's—and sprained both of her wrists, cracked a couple ribs. All that, and Daddy said she didn't even cry out." He held up one finger. "Not once, Marcus. Not a single scream." He shook his head, craned his head back around to stare up at that second story window. "Daddy was just a boy. Must'a scared him somethin' awful."

CHAPTER SIX
Gabriel, 1939

I woke to the sound of glass breaking.

I thought it was part of my dream at first. It was the day Natalie pushed Momma down the basement stairs all over again, but it weren't Nat that done it this time. It was me. I knew that. Knew it was me somehow, 'cause Momma was still falling, and I was standin' at the top of them steps, my arms still out, my palms facing down toward her. But things was different. The basement stairs was much too long. They stretched down and down, like they wasn't just reachin' to the basement but even further, somewhere deep down into the earth. And they wasn't no walls holdin' her in, neither, just blackness on both sides. I watched her tumble down those impossibly long stairs, getting smaller and smaller the further she fell, the jars she'd been carrying spilling from her arms, and I just knew she was dead this time. Like the time when Nat had shoved her had been the dream and this was real. I knew Momma was gonna die, but all I could do was watch. She fell and fell, glass jars sliding from her hands, and as much as I wanted to look away, as much as I knew I was 'bout to watch my momma meet her death, I just stood there and waited. She fell for a long, long time. I braced myself in the dream, felt myself tense up, waiting for the impact. Waitin' for her screams to cut off. It's like when you throw a penny in a wishing well and you cock your head to see iffin you can hear when it hits the water. I wished and wished I could take it back, that I wouldn't have to see what was happenin', but I was powerless, the way you are in dreams sometimes. When she got near the bottom (and I knew she was near the bottom, though I couldn't see nothin' down in that faraway darkness), I stopped breathing. And not in the dream this time, neither, I mean my body lying in my bedroom stopped breathing. She was tumbling, falling, crying out with every step she hit, bones breakin' on the wood, jars flying and crashing down in that darkness and then—

I sat up with a start. Breath hitchin' in my chest; Eyes squeezed tight. Glass was breakin' somewhere close. Jelly jars meeting the hard concrete floor of the basement. Momma breakin' down there, too.

I gripped my sweat-soaked sheet in my hands and squeezed, waited to hear one more cry from Momma. But it never came, just more shatterin' glass. I blinked once, twice, forced my eyes open all the way. My senses was just startin' to wake up alongside me, and that's when I heard it again. Faint but unmistakable. Someone was movin' around in the bedroom next to me and Mikey's. Nat's bedroom.

Another tinkling of glass, a few light footfalls. Pieces of my dream still stickin' in my brain, I suppose. Didn't know iffin it was real or not, just wakin' from one nightmare into the next, and for a moment, I couldn't move at all, part of me still standin' at the top of them long stairs. The moonlight shone in through my window in a sheet of silver across my bed, and I could see my toes stickin' out from the blanket. I wiggled 'em back and forth. For some reason, that's when I realized I weren't dreamin' no more. I tried to shake away the sleep that was still hanging heavy in my head, and I listened. At first, there weren't nothin'. The house was quiet. I had my window open about halfway, enough to let in the cool night breeze, and the night outside was just as calm and quiet. Then, sounds from the next bedroom; a soft crunching. Not glass shattering so much as broken glass being crushed underfoot. Then a grunt. A pause. Then another grunt, a little louder. Comin' from outside, now. Outside my window. Down in the back yard.

I gotta wake Mikey, I thought. One of the animals had gotten loose, and there'd be hell to pay if Pop Howard found out I'd heard 'em running around and didn't tell nobody. I glanced over to Mikey's bed, but he wasn't movin' under his blanket. I knew I should say something, but things was all mixed up in my head. I was still hearin' Momma's cries; the sounds of her body hitting them stairs. So instead, I forced myself all the way up to the edge of the bed, made myself put my feet on the floor. My legs was wet cement. I didn't wanna go to the window, didn't wanna see what was out there making them sounds. Every step was like I was walkin' underwater. The night was still, and I could hear more of them noises out there. A grunt, then a rasping, rattlin' breath. A grunt, then another breath. My own breath was as shaky as my legs, but I made myself walk to that window. I made myself look.

The silver light coating our bedroom made the backyard near as bright as daylight, and that's when I saw her—Natalie. Sixteen feet down and halfway across the yard already, dragging herself through the grass. Draggin', cause her left leg trailed behind her, her foot dangling lame and useless. Black spots was bloomin' all over her white gown. Blood seepin' through the fabric. She took these lurching, stuttering steps away from the house, grunting with the effort of it, her breath ripping out of her with each one. She sounded like a wounded animal, like a gutshot coyote. Not like my little sister. I didn't know how she was even still standin', but she was. She looked so small from up above. Such like the child she was. She drug herself across the yard, makin' her way toward the pond, and when I looked there, a shiver ran down my back.

She weren't alone out there in the night.

There was a man standing in the pond. No—on the pond. Right out in the middle, standing right on top that green water like Jesus Christ hisself. A near-black silhouette against the moonlit surface of the pond.

He was tall, balding on top, with long white hair that came from the sides of his head and fell well past his shoulders. A big, mangy beard that come down to his chest. Bone-thin.

Eyes like pits that reached straight to Hell.

He had one hand reaching out toward Natalie, like he was calling to her, like he was a suitor at the harvest festival asking her to dance.

Come, that hand was sayin'. Come to me.

She went.

Now I needed to wake Michael. I needed to yell and scream, needed Pop and Momma to come runnin', to sprint down there and save her, save my sister. She was hurtin' already, but this man, he was aimin' on hurtin' her some more. I knew that, sure as anything. There was a darkness around him that ain't have nothin' to do with the night, and one look at those pits for eyes, and I knew he wanted to wrap that darkness around her like a burial shroud and never let her go. Make her disappear. But it was the dream all over again. I was stuck there at that window like I had my feet nailed to the floorboards at the top of them basement stairs. It was like someone else was inside me— something else controlling me. I could feel my hands on the windowsill, my feet on the wooden floor, knew I was breathin', but I couldn't do nothin'. All I could do was stand there and watch. Witness.

Nat didn't stop when her feet hit that water. She waded in, never slowin' even a little. The water rose to her ankles, her knees, her waist. It pushed her gown up around her, and where the fabric soaked through, it clung to her skinny, broken body. The man didn't move, just watched her with those holes for eyes, still holding that withered hand out toward her. Nat lifted her own hand. Something glinted in the moonlight.

Glass. A shard of glass as long as her forearm. A piece from her busted window, no doubt. She was clutching it so tightly there was blood dripping from between her fingers. It sheeted down her hand, down her arm to the crook of her elbow. As still as the night was, as quiet as the country can be when it's asleep, I could hear it spattering into the water even from where I stood. Drip, drip, drip. How much blood is there inside a little girl? How much had she lost already? She swayed back and forth in front of the man, holding onto that glass like it was a crucifix, and my own hands clung tighter to the windowsill.

The man raised his hand a little higher. Nat raised her own, like she was gonna stab him or defend herself with that piece of glass shakin' in her hand. The man didn't flinch away, though. He never even blinked. Instead, he lifted his hand even higher, well up above his head, and Nat did the same. Like she was his reflection. Like she was his own pale shadow.

Only then did the man standing on top of the pond show any emotion.

He smiled. It was a horrible thing.

Then he made a fist with that hand, and quick as a whip, he slammed it into his stomach.

Nat's hand fell to her own stomach, and the glass tore through her dress and into the tender flesh beneath. She grunted, but she did not scream. She never screamed once. Again, the man lifted his own hand, and again he drove it into himself, and Natalie mirrored him. Up and down, up and down. So fast. So violent. The brittle glass tearing through her, into her, over and over, her hand gripping it so tightly it tore through her fingers, down into the bone. But she kept on, stabbing so hard the glass crumbled in her hands with every thrust, the gown tatters in mere seconds, the skin beneath just ribbons. Blood poured out of her now, gushing into that black water, mixing with it until it I couldn't tell what was blood and what was water and what was shadow, and it was all black as the sky above, as black as the water at the bottom of a well. The whole earth was bleeding, and my little sister was the wellspring.

Still, she did not scream. Not once. But someone did.

I watched as my little sister tore herself to pieces, and then something broke inside me, and I was screamin' and screamin' until my lungs felt like they was bleeding, and the blood vessels in my eyes felt like they would burst. I screamed for Michael, for Pop, for Momma. For Jesus. I screamed for Natalie. But no one seemed to hear. No one, but the man standing on top the pond.

Natalie collapsed after a dozen or so cuts. She fell to her knees in that bloody water, her head lolling to the side, the fight all but gone from her. Her life running out her stomach by the quart. But the man in the pond wasn't lookin' at her no more. His head had turned upward. He was lookin' at the house, at the open window on the second story. He was lookin' right at me.

I stopped screamin' when I saw that, when those two black holes bore into me.

Then I heard the voice. His voice.

I didn't hear it the way I had heard that blood drippin' down into the water.

I didn't hear it with my ears.

I heard it in my mind.

It was the voice of something dead or something dying, the words just so many chunks of broken ice being forced up through rotted vocal cords, being pushing out between decaying lips. It was the voice of the grave. And it knew me.

Jump, Gabriel, that voice said. Jump, and come to me.

One moment, I was standing at that windowsill unable to move, and the next I had one leg hanging out the side, dangling in the moonlight. Jumping would be an easy thing. There was nothing else I wanted more. To jump, to fall, to wade out into that cool water until I felt it's gentle kiss upon my skin. Until I felt that wasted hand upon my forehead. Anointing me. It was all right there in front of me. I just had to have faith. I just had to jump.

Hands gripped my shoulders. Fingers pressing down to the bone. And then I was falling, tumbling back inside the bedroom. My shoulders hit first. My neck snapped back and my head slammed into the floorboards. All the air in my lungs rushed out of me in a single, gaspin' breath. My lips moved but no words could come out, no air left in me to form them. I couldn't see nothin'.

A hand came down and slapped me across the cheek. Hard. Tears stung the corners of my eyes, but my lungs was working again, at least, and I could see again. Michael was bent over me. His eyes were wide in the moonlight. He had his right hand cocked back, ready for another slap.

"What the hell you doin, Gabe?" he shouted.

Kill him, Gabriel. Kill him.

A snapping of fingers in front of my face.

"Gabe, Gabe, look at me!"

Dig your nails into his eye sockets. Rip out his throat—

Hands on my shoulders again, shaking me.

—with your teeth. Kill him, and come to me.

I opened my mouth. It would feel good to sink my teeth through the skin of his naked throat. The warmth of his flesh. The saltiness of his blood as it ran out my open mouth—

Another slap, and then my ears was ringing. The voice was gone. I started crying all at once. I rolled over, curled my legs up against my chest. I couldn't look at Mikey. I felt like all the warmth I'd ever felt in my whole life had just left me, and now there was only cold and ash and darkness. I couldn't speak none, even if I'd wanted to. Michael was on his feet already anyway. I heard him rush to the window, and then he was screaming, too, running past where I was layin' and on out into the hallway. The house erupted with sound a moment later. I listened to the rumble of footsteps thundering down the hall, the back door opening and slammin' shut. The screams all outside now, far away. Water splashing. My momma's broken cries.

I got to my feet, and I staggered out into the hallway. I did not look toward the window. I didn't wanna see what was down in that water. My sister's body. That thing lookin' back up at me.

By the time I got to the kitchen door, Pop was haulin' Nat into the back of our Model A. They'd tied a sheet around her middle, but it was already a brilliant red, completely soaked through. Momma got in the front, then they was tearing down the driveway. Michael came around the corner a moment later, skin white as pearl, eyes red. Haggard, that's what he looked like. Scared. His longjohns had dark, angry stains all across the chest. I felt like weeping.

He pushed past me and fell into a chair, leaned his elbows on the kitchen table and rested his head in his hands. They was stained red, too, like the bedsheet, like Natalie. I sat next to him.

"Did ya see him, Mikey?" I asked, after a moment.

"Who?" he grunted without lookin' at me.

"The man. The man with the white hair."

He raised his head, narrowed his eyes.

"The man out there in the water," I tried again.

When he spoke, his voice was thin but hard. His hands was shakin' just the slightest.

"Ain't no one out there, Gabe. No man, anyways. Just Nat." He gave a jerky shake of his head, tried to smile. "What was left of her, at least." He looked back down to the table.

That numbness I had felt upstairs, that infernal cold, it was all gone now. Anger surged through my veins, and I felt my face grow hot.

"I saw him, dammit!" I slammed a hand on the table. "I saw him right out there in the pond. He was…he was doin' something to her. Makin her… makin' her hurt herself. I saw him, Mikey. I did."

Michael raised his head again. He was crying. He wouldn't look at me, just stared at a space just over my shoulder. At the door that led out into the backyard.

"No, Gabe, ain't no one out there." His voice cracked a little when he said out there. "I'da saw him if there was."

I leaned in a bit closer. I'd never seen Mikey cry, least not since we was smaller, and I didn't quite know what to do about it. Or why he was crying now. It didn't feel like it was just 'cause Natalie was hurt, though it could'a been. It made me feel like she died out there. Like we was already at her funeral.

My throat tried to close up, but I wouldn't let it.

I whispered, "Then tell me why you're so scared for."

Only then did he look at me, and I almost wished he hadn't. The blacks in his eyes looked a little too familiar.

"She told me she saw him, too, Gabe. That man with the white hair. Nat told me she saw Mr. Trench."

My mind went blank. Mr. Trench.

And then it hit me. Momma and the basement stairs. My dream. My waking nightmare.

Mikey reached a bloody hand out, gripped my wrist.

"I scooped her up out that water, and I swear she weren't barely breathing. I lift her up, put my ear to her chest to see if her heart was still beating, and when her head fell against my own, she whispered, *I saw him, Mikey. I saw Mr. Trench.*" Michael squeezed his eyes closed, but the tears kept coming.

He pulled his shirt up and wiped them away. "I told her to hush up, you know. I told her we was gonna get her some help and get her all fixed up, so she needed to hush up and rest. But right afore she passed out, she said it again. *I saw Mr. Trench, Mikey,* she said. *He was beautiful.*" Mikey looked back up to me, his eyes ringed red. "Then her body went limp in my arms, and she didn't say nothin' else."

His face collapsed in on itself, and then his head was back in his hands, and his whole body was shakin'. I ran and grabbed a handkerchief and gave it to him, then I sat next to him again and put my arms around him, and then we was both crying. Cryin' for Natalie, yes, of course, but there was something else, too, though I couldn't quite put my finger on it. It was something bigger than me, maybe bigger than all of us. Some evil thing, some darkness, it was spreading beneath us, beneath the whole farm. It was that same darkness I saw around the man in the pond. It terrified me. We sat that way for a while, until the sun started coming up, until we was all but done cried out.

Mikey sat back, and I did the same. I felt empty. Not just of warmth and happiness, like I had been up in the bedroom, but empty of everything. Hollow. Mikey sniffed and wiped at his eyes. Then, he got a curious look over him.

"What is it?" I asked.

"You, uh…y-you ever heard Pop talk about the Cellar Man before, Gabe? He ever bring that up to ya?"

I shook my head slowly. "No, never," I said. "Why?"

Mikey chewed at his lip, his eyes faraway again. He shook his head. I didn't think he was gonna say nothin'. But after a few moments, he did.

"It's prolly nothin, but…just after we got Nat in the car, right afore they took off, I heard him say something to Momma, that's all." He shook his head again, then he looked right at me, his eyes glossing over.

"He's back, he told her. The Cellar Man's back."

CHAPTER SEVEN

Uncle Pete tapped his fingers against the side of his can. Some of the color had drained from his face, and dark rings had begun to form under his arms and around the collar of his shirt. My own shirt started to feel a little tight, so I gripped it up near the collar and fanned it in and out a few times.

"Natalie was in the hospital for nearly two weeks. Poor thing was all tore up. The only silver lining is that the glass in them upstairs windows was old and thin and brittle. Her belly had been cut up real good, but by some saving grace, she had missed her organs. Still, the damage was something awful… hardly any skin left to stitch back together. Must'a lost a gallon of blood out there, too. She was never the strongest of kids anyway, and the whole ordeal seemed to take something from her, something other than just the blood and the tears and the broken bones. When they brought her home, she was just all dried out. Frail. A husk.

"They ain't know what to do with her. She needed to stay in bed…even just walkin' around would have been enough to rip open everything the doctors had sewed up. They couldn't rightly leave her in her room, neither, not with everything that had happened."

A fragment of a memory came to me then, a piece of my childhood that had been sunk into the bottom of my consciousness like a sack of kittens into a deep river. And now, that muddy bottom had been dredged up by all this talk of family and history and tragedy. I remembered now—where I'd heard that voice. The one that seemed to only surface when I was at The Roost. The door to the basement steps flashed in my mind, and with it came a long-forgotten memory.

I was eleven years old, standing in the kitchen of the farmhouse, edging my way toward the door that led into the basement. I was a nervous kid anyway, but doing something I wasn't allowed to do made me all jittery, made my face glow hot. I wasn't allowed in the basement, same as the pond. But the thing was, I didn't *want* to go. I didn't want to, but I *had* to. There was someone down there, I was sure. A voice—a little girl's voice, scared and whispy and as brittle-thin as pencil lead—had called out my name from the other side of the door. *Marcus*, it said. *Marcus, I'm so scared. It's so dark down here, and...and he's comin' for me.* I had my hand on the doorknob before I knew what I was doing, had it half-turned when Aunt Laurie came into the kitchen. Her face turned an ugly shade of red; her eyes narrowed to slits.

The thing about my Aunt Laurie is she was one of the kindest, sweetest, good-hearted people I've ever come across in my life. One of those rare grownups who knows how to talk to a kid without talking down to them. One who knew how to listen. But when I saw her face change, saw that smile wilt on her face, and that red exploding in her cheeks, I felt my stomach drop. It was the only time I ever saw her get angry. It was the first time I ever saw a grownup be afraid.

She yelled. I don't remember what. Aunt Laurie never yelled. I was so startled I began to cry almost immediately. Her face shattered. The anger fell away in pieces. She rushed to me and crouched down, wrapped her arms around me. She held me then, patted the back of my head, quietly whispered into my ear. She extracted promises from me between words of love and forgiveness, made me promise never to touch that doorknob again, to never even *think* of going down in the basement. Before I ran back outside, I saw that Aunt Laurie had been crying, too. Her red eyes never left that heavy wooden door.

"They kept her in the basement, didn't they."

To his credit, Uncle Pete didn't look surprised, though I swore I saw his upper lip twitch a bit. He sighed.

"That's right. Yeah, that's just right. They kept her in the basement." He cocked his head at me.

"You never been down there, have you?" I shook my head.

"Didn't think so. Well, there's a small room in the back there, nothin' but shelves along the walls and a single lightbulb hanging from a wire in the middle. The canning room is what they called it, where Grandma Lenore kept all her canned vegetables and preserves she had stored up. Hardly bigger than a closet, really, but there weren't no windows, and only one door, and after Howard took down a few shelves, he was able to fit a small bed in there, though it was a bit tight. Really just a jail cell; a jail cell with stone walls instead of bars, but a cell all the same. But they was just tryin' to keep her safe. You see that, don't ya? Wanted to keep them all safe. But this place here, The Roost, it…it weren't made to keep things safe. It just ain't in its nature.

"Things were different around here after that. With little Natalie shut away deep in the basement, it seemed the rest of the family found it hard to get back in a normal routine. Pop Howard was angry most of the time. He stalked around the yard like a guard in a labor camp, lookin' for someone to pistol-whip. Didn't talk to nobody. He stayed out the house from sunup until sundown. Lenore tried to talk to him at first, but all she ever got out of it was a few harsh words and fresh tears. She had changed, too, though, and not for the better. She sank into herself. She walked around the house like a ghost drifting from room to room. She'd enter a room and stand perfectly still like she was listening to something, to some softly playing music no one else could hear. She hummed under her breath in broken melodies, bible hymns she hadn't heard since she was a girl. Her hands shook so much she could hardly pass the butter at the dinner table without knocking something over. She hardly noticed Daddy, but she absolutely refused to go down in the basement. She never really forgave Natalie for pushing her down them stairs, not really. She never thought it was no accident. But this—*this* sealed the deal. Far as she was concerned, she only had two boys left.

"Michael, he got near as bad as Howard. When they'd first brought Natalie home from the hospital, he'd agreed with his parents. He thought the basement was just about the safest place for her. He took it in his mind he was her protector. He's the one that fed her every day. He went down and sat with her at every meal, checked in on her in between. He'd bring her favorite books and her favorite dolls and smuggled cookies fresh off the pan before they even cooled. He'd read to her when she was too weak to lift her head. He'd hold her hand and tell her about his day, how his job down at the Hilborn Feed & Grain was going. He'd talk to her for hours, even when she seemed to be sleeping. Anything to help bring her spirits up. To help her heal. It weren't no easy thing. That basement room with those dirt walls…Christ, it was a depressing sight. No sunlight, just the feeble glow of a single light bulb. A bulb like that, hanging in the center of the ceiling, it casts shadows in all directions. The room was more shadow than light. And the walls…they cut off any sound from the house above. The dirt and stone held the moisture of the earth in it, and the earth down there, it's always cold. Every breath was like inhaling cool water into your lungs. And you could hear every breath, that's the thing, the thing that would just about drive you crazy. There weren't no other sounds inside those four walls, not when Natalie was alone. Just the voices that like to talk back and forth inside your head for company. That room kept Natalie safe, *physically* safe. But up here," Uncle Pete said, pointing to his head. "Up here, she started slipping away, even worse than before.

"My daddy was twelve at the time, and I think he had it the worst of all of them. Besides his sister, that is. Everyone else had changed, and he was…well, he was mostly forgotten. Left on his own, kinda like an orphan who still lived with his family. He was too young to get a job in Hilborn, so most of the time he was here. Before and after school, he had his chores to keep him busy, but it wasn't like it had been. Howard wouldn't pay him no mind, and his momma hardly noticed him. Michael is what really hurt him though. They'd been as thick as thieves most their lives. Just a few years apart, you know, and like little boys is wont to do, he idolized his older brother. Until all this shit, they'd spent most they time together. Exploring the woods, sloshing through the Honey catching frogs, picking through the freshly plowed fields to look for arrowheads…yeah, Daddy was Michael's shadow for most his life. But what's a shadow when it gets disconnected from the thing the light's shining on? Any free time Michael had now, he'd be spending it downstairs with Natalie. Daddy went down there, too, but it was different for him. It scared him, to tell the truth. Seeing her all bandaged up the way she was, her blonde hair pasted against her forehead. And the smell, Marcus…it hit you before you even got all the way down the steps. Not her fault, of course, bedridden as she was. But you take all the smells of a hospital room, the piss and the shit in the bedpan, the old food, the antiseptic of the medicine. Not to mention the overall scent of sickness, of a body not right on the inside. But hospital rooms have windows, they have fresh air and sunlight and a staff of people working 'round the clock, changing bedding and bandages and cleaning the place. You can't polish a stone wall or a cement floor. Yeah, it scared Daddy going down there. It'd scare any kid. And Natalie, she…she wouldn't talk to nobody but Michael anyway. Howard had the yard, and Lenore had the house, and Michael and Natalie had the basement. So, what'd that leave for Daddy?

"He was just a kid, but he felt responsible for what had happened for some reason. Maybe 'cause he seen't her first, that night, down by this pond. Maybe he thought he coulda stopped her iffin he'd been quick enough. That he coulda changed things. Or, maybe, he just did what most kids do when things in their life turn sideways and the reasons are too big for them to really wrap their heads around it—he blamed himself.

"The next day, after Natalie had her incident, when she was still at the hospital, Daddy went looking for the man. Mr. Trench—the Cellar Man, whatever you wanna call him. Daddy wanted to track him down. He thought that could make things better, thought maybe it would turn things back the way they was. He went round and round the pond first, looking for boot prints in the soft ground along the water, for a lost glove or a hat, a scrap of cloth stuck in the brambles. When he didn't find nothin', he walked along the banks of the Honey with his pocketknife in his hand, searching the mud on both sides of the river. He combed the woods to the west, checked the furrows in the fields to the east. He checked somewhere different nearly every day. I don't have to tell you, Marcus, but there was nothing. Not a sign. The man—if there was a man—had came and gone like a puff of smoke."

I looked out to the steadily dwindling pond, right out at the center where Grandpa Gabe had first spotted the man seemingly standing on the water, and the skin on my arms raised up in a rash of goosebumps. Grandpa had just been a boy. Scared to death at the sight of the stranger in the water, but also at the violence of the act. His little sister, cutting herself, over and over. The blood raining down into the pond. And yet, even with his family falling apart around him, he had went looking for that man, that stranger. That demon. And he had done it alone. Christ, had I ever been challenged that way in my entire life? Had I ever had to dig to find such strength of will inside myself? I didn't think so.

I thought of Dad floating out there, of the call from Uncle Pete telling me what had happened. Of the numb feeling that had started in my stomach and spread out to every finger, every toe, to every part of me until it rushed back in one great wave to still my heart, even before I had put the phone down.

It hadn't been easy. I won't pretend that it was. I don't think it matters what age you are; losing a parent, one that you loved and one that loved you, is one of the hardest things you'll ever have to go through. It's not just the fact you've lost someone close to you. It's so much more. No one has known you as long as your parents, and even when you've gone through the radical changes of puberty, the tumult of your teens, the shaky transition into adulthood, even when you think you've changed so much, no one knows you more completely than your parents. For every story they ever told you about your childhood, for every memory shared that you yourself had long forgotten (or never bothered to remember), for every picture that they and they alone knew the backstory of, there were a thousand more things they never told you. The feelings that they felt when they saw you growing up. The apprehension, the worry, the strain of parenting, of being responsible for someone else's life. The pains to teach you, to love you, to care for you unconditionally while still being just a human being themselves, while still being flawed, while still not knowing exactly what to do in every situation, not being sure what was going on in their own lives. All the time invested, all the smiles and the laughter. All the fears, and tears, and heartache. The simple joy of doing a thing that is never simple. All this is just to say, when you lose a parent, you lose pieces of yourself you never even knew you had until they were ripped away from you. Pieces of your foundation, the things that built you up and kept you stable. And you never realize they're there until they're gone, and you feel like you're collapsing on the inside.

So no, it hadn't been easy when Dad died. The years since it happened had been a balm, a haphazardly applied bandage. But the wound hadn't healed. It might never. I made the best peace I could with that. Sometimes, just surviving is the strongest thing you can do.

But to be a boy, to have your whole family ripped away at once…even if they were all still alive, to go through all of that and still stand up, still try to make things right, that was a different kind of strength. I saw the two parts of my Grandpa Gabe, then, both the boy with vengeance in his heart, and the old man, half-naked and curled up on the ice, still searching.

I reached a hesitant hand out to where Uncle Pete was sitting. He flinched when I touched his shoulder, but relaxed when he saw it was just me. His own calloused palm clamped over top of my hand and squeezed.

"Thanks," he choked out.

"Yeah."

He patted my hand twice, and I took that as a signal to pull it back into my lap. We were both uncomfortable with being comforted, it seemed. It was a Castle trait, through and through.

"Getch'a a beer?" he asked.

"One step ahead of you," I said, opening the lid to the cooler. The ice inside was half-melted and floating in a few inches of cold water, and I wondered, in my half-buzzed state, if the pond and the cooler were on opposite sides of some equation, like the more the pond drained, the more the cooler filled with water. Christ, the beers were hitting me harder than

I had realized. Maybe it was just the novelty of not drinking alone in my apartment. It was kind of hard to tell exactly how fucked up you were when you didn't have to talk, didn't have to listen or react. When you passed out alone and woke up the same way. *Shut up, asshole.* I slid a fresh can to Uncle Pete, and he thanked me. He cracked it open and guzzled, draining half the can in a single go. I did the same, tomorrow's hangover be damned.

"Now," Pete said, shifting in his chair. "Now we get to the part of the story that ain't so easy to tell."

I barked out the first note of a laugh before I knew I was doing it.

"Has any of this shit been easy?"

"Fuck no, it ain't." He smiled. "But if the fields of Hell are plowed with all our sins and suffering, then, boy, we just barely dug our hoes into the soil."

He let that hang out there in the space between for a few pauses.

"It might seem like things was really bad, lockin' a little girl away like that. And they was. But for a little while, they all felt like maybe things could turn around. That she was safe. That they all were. Daddy was shook up, but he thought the worst was behind them." Uncle Pete sucked at his teeth. "No one more optimistic than a child, I guess. A lot of good it did him."

CHAPTER EIGHT

Gabriel, 1939

The Roost was always quiet now, but it weren't a peaceful kind of quiet. Not like some place long abandoned, a place that had time to get used to bein' empty. This were a restless kind of quiet; a house of the dead where the ghosts ain't know where they was supposed to go yet. That's what I felt like most days, just a ghost. Pop never got after me to get my chores done no more, and Momma flitted from room to room, her bare feet never making a sound, her eyes never quite focusin' in on me when she talked. Not that she had much to say to me, either way. Didn't seem like no one had nothin' much to say to each other anymore.

It was easier just to stay in me and Mikey's room, to stay out the way of everyone walkin' around like they guts was missin'. Maybe, I thought, if I kept myself hidden away, then maybe someday Momma would look up—really look up, look around her—and see I was gone. Maybe she'd wonder where I been. Maybe she'd wanna talk to me, or hug me, tell me everything was gonna be okay again. But it ain't worked yet. The house stayed as quiet as a funeral parlor. That's why the fear hit me straight away when I heard the voices comin' up through the floorboards like old dust.

Loud voices. Had to be if I was hearin' it all the way up through my closed door. One moment, I was just layin' on my bed, tryin' not to think of too much, 'cause too much of what I been thinkin' on lately was painful things. The next moment, there comes these loud noises like distant thunder from downstairs, and my stomach's twisting up in knots, and my heart is hammerin' inside me like I just got done runnin' down the driveway. Fear, but excitement, too, all mixed up together. I sat up, quick, crossed over to the door, eased it open, tiptoed down the hall, every step like I was walkin' on needles.

I paused at the top of the steps. My fingers was trembling on the banister as I listened.

"She's dyin' down there!" Michael was screamin'. "She's dyin' slow, and ya'll don't even care!"

"We gotta keep her safe, Michael," Momma said. She sounded bone-tired. "She can't be left alone to her own devices. You know that. You know what happened."

"Well, it ain't right. Ya'll treatin' her like a goddam criminal!"

"Michael Joseph Castle, don't you dare take the Lord's name in vain inside this house!"

"God ain't in this house, Momma! He ain't been here in a long time. Can't you feel that? Can't you feel the…the emptiness? He's gone. You and Pop, y-you drove him out. This here's the devil's house, now. And I know exactly who he's workin' his will through."

The sound of the slap echoed up the stairs, bouncing off the walls of the hallway. I flinched, but I ain't dare move none. My feet stayed stuck to the floorboards like they had roots growin' through 'em. For a few awful moments, the silence coming from downstairs was even louder than that slap. The whole house seemed to be holdin' its breath, and I held mine right along with it.

The next words was so soft I barely caught 'em. Mikey—but not like I'd ever heard him.

"You gonna get what you got comin to ya, Momma. You and Pop both. When God does show his face 'round here, you two gonna get your just rewards. I promise ya that."

The front door slammed shut, and then the house went back to that quiet I'd grown so accustomed to. That ghostly quiet, only interrupted by the sound of the tickin' clock in the dining room, and a soft, gentle sobbing. I tiptoed back to my room as best as I could, though I was cryin' now, too. It scared me somethin' awful, the way Mikey had talked to Momma. The hatred in his voice. None of us kids had ever talked to her or Pop that way, no way. There was some things you just knew not to do lest you wanted to feel the backside of a hand or the bite of Pop's whippin' stick. But there was some sickness here now, in The Roost, some malady creepin' through the walls and restin' up on the roof, some disease seepin' into each of us. It made Pop near inconsolable with anger, made Momma as gray and dull as a thick mornin' fog. Poor Natalie was shut away downstairs, might as well have been in a whole other house altogether. Mikey, who I'd always been so close with, had pulled away from me, pulled away from all of us save for Nat.

I got on my knees next to my bed, and I clasped my hands together and closed my eyes. I ain't prayed in so long, not since Nat went out the bedroom window. Mikey had been right about that, at least. God weren't hangin' around The Roost no more. It felt like I was tryin' to talk to a stranger. But I tried anyway. I prayed for my family to come back together, the way we used to be. I prayed that Nat would get better, that whatever was hauntin' her mind would leave her be, leave us all be. That I would wake up in the mornin' and go down to breakfast and they would all be sittin' there, Nat, too, and we'd all be lookin' 'round the table at each other, kinda sheepish, a bit red-faced but lookin' at each other, really lookin', seein' each other for the first time in a long time, and then we'd all kinda laugh and shrug it off and start passin' plates 'round, tellin' small jokes and makin' plans and just lookin' forward to another day, like a real family does.

Whether or not there was anyone listenin' to me, I felt better when I got up off the floor. Lighter. Things was gonna be different. They was gonna be good again.

I DON'T KNOW how Pop found out about what went on between Momma and Mikey. Ain't like they was talkin' much either anymore, and as pissed as he was these days, always grumbling to hisself, always stayin' away from the house, it weren't like he woulda noticed how Momma was all tore up over it. Mikey wouldn't-a told him neither. But someone did, that's for certain. 'Cause he found out.

I was over in the cornfield when I heard the screams. I came runnin', but I was almost too late.

Pop had Mikey up against the garage right next to the window, his fingers wrapped around his throat, pinnin' him to the siding. His other fist was cocked back, big as a ham, the knuckles already bloody. Mikey was as helpless as a baby. He was clawin' at Daddy's hand, tryin' to scream but he could hardly breathe. Blood flooded down out his nose, mixin' with the tears and the snot and the dirt on his face. His cheeks was an ugly purple, already swellin' up.

"N-no!" Mikey managed to choke out right before that fist came down and socked him in his right eye. His head bounced back, slammed into the garage. It made a hollow sound that made me sick. Pop's hand on his throat never moved none though, held Mikey firm. Held him straight. He weren't sayin' nothin', and that was almost worse than iffin he'd been yellin'. Mikey was struggling, tryin' to scream again, but all that came out was a wet yelp. Pop cocked his fist back again, and when he punched, Mikey managed to shift his head a bit so the blow glanced off his swollen cheek rather than hittin' him square in the nose. I'm sure Mikey woulda fell down then, iffin he could, iffin he wasn't held up by that steel-stiff arm, stuck the way he was. His eyes was nearly swole shut. He moved his head back and forth best he could, tryin' to avoid that fist, wantin' to scream but there wasn't no air left in his lungs. Tryin' to get through to Pop, that's what I think. Tryin' to reason with him without words. But it weren't no use. Pop's eyes was as black as the bottom of the well, and he wasn't seein' Mikey at all.

I was gonna watch my brother die. I was gonna stand here while Pop beat the life out of him. And there was nothin' I could do.

Momma came racin' around the corner, already screamin', tears fallin' down her face.

"Howard! Howard!" she was screamin'. "Leave him go, Howard, just leave him go."

Pop didn't turn, didn't even pause before layin' into Mikey one more time, this one hittin' him straight in the gut.

Momma ran up to Daddy, got both hands on his cocked-back fist. She was wailing now, praying, I think, all *pleases* and *Gods* and *Lords* and *mercies*, but I was cryin' too, now, and I could hardly hear her above the blood beatin' a war drum in my head. Pop Howard was a bull of a man, not too tall but thick as an ox, hard-packed muscle from a lifetime of baling hay and plowin' and wrestling ornery livestock into their pens. Momma ain't have a chance, but she tried. He got in another punch, then another, the whole time Momma just hangin' onto that arm. Seein' her there did something to me though, the way her thin frame clung to that mountain of a man, and I ran forward. I got myself between Pop and Mikey, shoved my way in until my back was to my brother, my arms spread out to the side. My eyes found Pop's fist, and I waited for it to come crashin' down, to slam into me the way it'd been slammin' into Mikey, to break the bones in my face, to crush me. But he weren't aimin' for me, and his fist found Mikey's nose again. I heard the cartilage crack like kindling, felt the hot spray of blood cross the back of my neck. Some of it sprayed out and hit Pop, hit him right in those black eyes. Only then did he seem to notice what was right in front of him. He blinked a few times, squeezing his eyes together hard like he was havin' some sort of headache. His shoulders sagged. His whole body seemed to go limp at once. He fell forward, and as he did the hand on Mikey's throat released him, and then we was all fallin' down to the ground, Pop and Momma and me and Michael, all in one big, screamin', sobbin' pile in the grass beside the garage.

"Howard," Momma was moanin'. "Oh, Howard. Oh, Howard…"

Michael was coughin'. He had rolled to his side, heavin' great big lungfuls of air into him, it comin' right back out. He threw up, gagged some more, then threw up again, his breath coming in great heavy whoops, not able to talk yet, just getting all that awfulness outta him.

Pop laid beside him in the grass, his eyes open but not fixed on nothin', just starin'. He was breathin' heavy, too. Momma was beside him on her knees, crouched over him, really prayin' this time, whatever good that would do. She held her hands over her eyes like she ain't wanna see what was right in front of her. Her shoulders was shakin'.

I was cryin', too, though I wasn't hurt none. I ain't the one been beaten, but I still felt that awfulness inside me. Cryin' seemed to get a bit of it out. We sat that way for a few minutes, cryin' and moanin' and prayin' all in turn. The wind had picked up, and the leaves of the dryin' corn stalks was whisperin' their discontent. The cows and the goat was agitated, and they was cryin' out, too, like they could sense something was wrong and they was scared of it.

And then, for just a couple seconds, we all took a breath. The people, the animals, the wind.

And that's when we heard the screamin'. Loud and full of terror so deep it shook us all out of our daze. It was comin' from inside the house.

Natalie.

I hadn't realized I said it out loud, but as soon as her name left my lips everyone started movin' at once. Michael sat up first, one eye completely swole shut, the rest of his face just covered in a mask of dryin' blood. He squinted toward the house with his other eye, toward that awful screamin'. "Nat," he grunted through his busted lips, and fresh blood trickled out the side of his mouth. Momma was on her feet, her hands under one of Pop's arms, tryin' to help him up. He got up slow, staggered a bit like he was drunk. His eyes was still unfocused. He didn't seem sure where he was exactly. I stood up, leaned down to help Mikey to his feet. His skin was burnin' up. Somehow, he stayed on his feet, though he was swayin' pretty bad. He took two steps toward the house, then Pop was there, that old fire back in his eyes.

I cried out. It was gonna happen again, and this time Pop weren't gonna stop. Me and Momma were no match for him. He was gonna finish what he started whether we got in his way or not. But Pop ain't throw a punch this time. He just held a finger in Mikey's face.

"You stay outta this," he said, in a growl. "You just turn your ass around and head for the road, y'hear me? You ain't got nothin' left to do with this family."

"P-pop, I'm s-sorry–' Michael started, but Pop shook him by his shirt.

"You shut up, boy. You just shut the hell up. You've said ya piece, and I ain't fixin' to hear no more of it. Bringing the devil down here." He spat at his feet. "Me and ya momma done worked our hands to the bone takin care of you three, and that's how ya say ya thanks? Sayin' we brought the devil down here?" His pointed finger closed, and his hand clenched into a fist.

He laughed, a short, brittle sound, then he shook his head. "You'll get the hell outta here, Michael, if ya know what's good for ya. This ain't ya home no more." He shoved Mikey, and Mikey fell back into the grass. Pop stalked toward the house without looking back. Momma looked back, just once, her face a mask though her eyes filled with fresh tears. She followed behind Pop anyway and never said nothin'. I ain't know what to do, who to follow, who to help. They was all pullin' me in different directions.

"Mikey," I said, barely just a whisper. "Y-you okay, Mikey?"

He coughed, more blood runnin' out his mouth.

"What's it look like?"

"I'm sorry, Mikey. I-I couldn't stop him. I wanted to, but I, I couldn't. He's just mad now, he'll…he'll change his mind. Ya just gotta let him cool off a bit."

Mikey stared at me with that one good eye, the whites just as blood red as the rest of his face. He spat out on the ground. It was all red.

"*Fuck* him."

I flinched. I looked back to the house, makin' sure that Pop and Momma was really gone.

"Don't say that, Mikey! What if he heard you? What if M-momma heard you?"

"Then, fuck her, too, Gabriel. Fuck this whole family."

Mikey pushed himself up with shaky arms and got to his feet. He was a complete mess, his face a patchwork of bloated purples and shiny, wet reds, swirls of yellow stitched around his eyes and his mouth. He looked like something dead, and if not dead yet, something well on its way down that road. He swayed a bit, like maybe if the wind picked up, he'd be blown right over. Then he straightened. He didn't say nothin', just turned and shuffled off toward the driveway, toward the road beyond it.

"Where ya goin, Mikey?"

"Away," he said, over his shoulder. "I'm goin' away. But I'll be back."

I GLANCED OVER to Uncle Pete. His eyes were closed. He could have just been sleepy, those handful of beers finally catching up to him, but I didn't think so. He was picturing it, seeing the whole thing playing out in his head. He was living it. I looked over to the garage, to that spot in the grass just below the window. I could almost see the blood there staining the green a vibrant crimson. I reached a hand out again to touch Pete's shoulder, but I thought better of it. Let sleeping dogs lie, and all that. I decided to say something instead, though I thought I already knew the answer.

"Did he come back?" I asked. "Did Michael ever come back here to The Roost?"

Uncle Pete opened his eyes. His mouth was set in a straight line.

"Oh yeah," he said, pushing the words through those closed lips. "He sure did. About three days later, he made his way back here.

"And then he never left again. At least, not all of him."

"When are you leaving?"

"Anna," he said over his shoulder. "I'm going away. But I'll be back."

I'd gone to see Uncle Viva. His eyes were closed. He could have just been sleeping, those hundreds of years finally catching up with him, but I think He was putting it so—the whole thing plummeted in his head. He was looking at—I looked over at the game, at that spot in the grass just by the window. I could almost see the blood there, taking the green a... I reached out again to touch her shoulder, but I thought better of it. Her sleeping dust—and then I decided to ask someone instead, though I already knew the answer.

"Did he come back, Lasete?" I asked. "Did Micmael ever come back here to the Kiosk."

Uncle Pele opened his eyes. His mouth was set in a straight line.

"Oh yeah," he said, pushing the words through clinched teeth. "He sure did. About three days later, he made his way back here.

"And then he never left again, Arcae," he called him."

CHAPTER NINE

Gabriel, 1939

Mikey came back to The Roost three days later. Snuck back like a horse thief in the middle of the night, when he knew everybody would be asleep. And everyone was. Everyone, except me.

Truth is, I ain't been sleeping too good since that awful night when Nat jumped out the window. Since she damn near killed herself. You see, I knew that man with the long hair was gonna come back. I was more sure of that than anything. When I'd seen him that night, floating above the water, seen the way he was lookin' at Nat while she tore herself up with that glass, I knew he wanted her dead. There was that darkness that surrounded him, you know, waiting to swallow her up. It was a hungry darkness. And that hunger wasn't gonna be satisfied until all the life had run out of her into that green water. But Nat was tougher than anyone gave her credit for. She was a fighter. She'd survived, somehow. And I knew it sure as sunshine that that man was gonna come back and snatch what was left of her if he could. If I let him.

So, most my nights I spent staring out my window, watching the night get darker and darker, watching the water of the pond get just as black as motor oil. If he came back—when he came back—I was gonna be ready for him. I ain't have no idea what exactly I would do iffin I saw him, but I wasn't gonna let him take anything else from us. I wasn't gonna let him back inside my head.

Makes me laugh even thinkin' it, cause the truth of it is, he's always in my head. Not the way he'd been that night, the way he'd made me feel like a goddam puppet with his hand up my back, controlling me, telling me to do things. But he was still there. I'd like to say I was up all night keeping my vigil out of some sense of honor or duty, and I suppose there was some of that mixed in, but mostly, it was fear. Fear to close my eyes in the darkness of my empty room. Because that awful night wasn't the last time I saw Mr. Trench, or the Cellar Man, or whoever he was. I'd seen him every single night since, as well.

He weren't outside, down by the pond. He was in my dreams. In my room. Right beside my bed.

Watching me with one gnarled hand reaching out.

I could chalk it up to just a nightmare. It had been the most horrible night of my life, after all. My little sister damn near dead. The violence of it. The blood. But when I opened my eyes that next night and saw that skeleton of a man hovering over me, it didn't seem like no nightmare I'd ever had. It was too real. He was too real. There were things about him I couldn't have seen from where I stood at the window. Details that had been hidden by the distance and by the night. But with him standing just a foot away from where I slept, I could see it all. And it was horrifying.

The skin beneath his scraggly beard was wrinkled and pruney, so white it was damn near see-through. It was like there weren't no fat or muscle under it, just bone. His cheeks sank inward, the flesh clinging so tightly his head weren't nothin' but a skull with hair, and those dead, empty eyes. The whites was blazing red, two coals left burning at the bottom of a pit of ash, the sockets themselves so hollow his flat, pancaked pupils seemed to be bugging out of his face. There was stuff growing there, too, I could see, right in the corners of those hollowed-out sockets. Black stuff. Looked like mold, maybe. The skin of a peach gone to rot in the summer heat. And Christ, he was skinny. Bone-thin. Mr. Morris down at the school showed us pictures of the POW's held in Andersonville, Georgia during the Civil War. Men starved for months and months until they bodies ate themselves. That's what that phantom looked like to me. Like he'd starved to death months ago, years ago, like his body had ate itself, and he was already decomposing but somehow he just didn't know, just kept living through it. That one gnarled hand he held out to me weren't nothing but the hand of a corpse. The middle three fingers was just stumps, cut down to the first knuckle, the bone peeking through all jagged and just as white as moonlight, what little flesh left there thin as paper.

And the smell. The smell, I think, is what made it too real for me. I could shake it all off and tell myself it was just a nightmare, that this apparition in my bedroom was just something that popped out of my head, but the smell made it real. The stink of it. Waterlogged wood and rotten meat, moldy potatoes and old blood. I'd close my eyes when he showed up. I'd shake my head and cover myself with my blanket. Usually, that would work. But even after the sun finally came up and I dared myself to look and found the bedroom empty, the smell would still be there. I can still smell it now.

When I saw Mikey crouching through the darkness at the edge of the yard, I was sure it was the man coming back for me. My fingers dug into the windowsill. My throat closed up like I had stitches in the back of my mouth. I couldn't scream, couldn't even back away. All this time spent wondering what I would do when he came back, and here I was as stuck to the floor as I had been the other night. Just as helpless. But the fear inside me slowed a bit when the walking shadow came into focus. It weren't tall enough for one. Not near as skinny. No long white hair catching what little moonlight was peeking from behind the clouds. When the shadow got closer, when it came around the side of the pond and I recognized Mikey, I let go of a long, shaky breath and I damn near laughed. It weren't no killer; it was just my brother.

But that brought a different kind of fear. Pop Howard. What the hell was Mikey doin' back here? There ain't no way he'd get a warm reception, at least not from Pop and Momma. Not after the way he left. Not after Pop damn near killed him. Was he crazy? Had he been touched by whatever had touched Nat? I shuddered at the thought. I been the one havin' to take Nat her meals ever since Michael left. She was still my little sister, banged up and stitched back the way she was, but there was something different about her now. It was in the way she looked at me when I came in with her dinner plate. Like she was older somehow. Like she was older than me. It gave me the willies, truth be told. What if Michael was like that now? I'd never felt more alone.

Mikey sloped through the yard, back bent, his feet not making a sound in the grass. He came right up to the house, right below my window. The lights was off, and the moon was barely there behind the clouds. Ain't no way he could see me watching him. Ain't no way he could hear me. But he stood there, right below me, head cocked up toward my window, just waiting. His face was still bruised pretty bad, the skin still swollen. But he looked okay. He was still my brother. But what was I so scared for? I shook my head, leaned out just a few inches. I was gonna hiss a warning to him, try to get him to see some sense, that there weren't nothing in this house for him right now but more heartache, more violence. But before I could say a word, he lifted a finger to his lips. He shook his head, and when he saw I weren't gonna say nothin', he smiled. I smiled back. God, but it was good to see him, even with the way things were. And then he was moving again. Movin toward the house, not back into the fields like I figured he'd do. He had a hand down at his side, and just before he disappeared into the shadow of the house, I saw something flash there, something he was holdin' tight too. Something he ain't want me to see. Something silver. There and then gone.

The fear came rushing back, so hard it nearly knocked me down to the floor. Something bad was gonna happen. Maybe something worse than what had already happened at The Roost. I braced myself, waitin' to hear the front door bang open. For the yelling to begin. The screams and the punches, furniture being thrown over or glass breakin'. Something was gonna happen, and I didn't want to hear it. But I couldn't stop listening. I crept over to my bedroom door and locked it, hoped it would hold when all hell broke loose in the house. I put my ear to the wood and waited. I waited a long while. But nothin happened. No silent footfalls in the hallway, no creak of floorboards or rushed whispering at the doorjamb. No whine of bedsprings comin' from Pop and Momma's bedroom. Nothin'. Had Mikey turned back at the last minute? Had he come to his senses and realized how foolish it was to be back here? I waited. I waited for a long time. And when I couldn't take it no more, when I couldn't just stand there like a man waitin' to hear the judge say he was to be hung in the town square, I sat in my bed. I wasn't gonna fall asleep this time. My guts was all twisted up, my head all full of bad ideas. I was gonna wait until I saw the sun peeking out above the trees, and then I was gonna go downstairs and see what the hell was goin' on. Just a few more hours, that's all.

I woke up with a start. Sunlight was streamin' in through my window. I'd fallen asleep sittin' up, my legs crossed, my head leaned back against the wall, and everything was sore. I winced as I leaned forward and scooted to the edge of the bed, my feet nearly numb from how I'd been sittin' there. Something was wrong. What had woken me up? I paused and listened.

There was movement somewhere in the house. Pop and Momma musta been awake for hours. But it weren't screaming or yelling. It weren't stuff breaking. And it should have been if Mikey had actually come back here. So where was he? Had it all been a dream?

I didn't wait this time. I couldn't take it anymore. I unlocked the door and crept down the hallway, sure I was gonna hear some commotion. But when I got to the top of the stairs, there was another surprise; the smell of a country breakfast cookin' away in the kitchen. I could hear the muffled sounds of pots clanging, of low conversation. And then, laughter. When was the last time I'd heard laughter ringing out under this roof? All the sudden I felt like crying. I ain't realize how much I missed that sound. I nearly ran down the stairs. It felt like Christmas mornin'.

When I turned the corner from the dining room and peered through the kitchen doorway, I froze. There was a plate of flapjacks on the counter, steam still rising from 'em, and a whole mess of sausages sizzling away on the stovetop. And there was Pop and Momma. Standing close to each other, closer than they had in weeks, since before the bad times. And they was smiling. He was leaned back against the counter, a cup of coffee in his hands, and she had a hand on the cast-iron pan. And they was smiling at each other. Not yelling. No dirty looks. No cold shoulder.

I couldn't say nothin', just stared. Momma noticed me first. She turned her head and saw me and she smiled even wider. My heart felt like a tiny sun in my chest. So long since she'd even noticed I was around. Her smile made her look ten years younger.

"Well, there you are, little one," she said. Little one. Hadn't called me that since I was seven or eight. "I was just about to come wake you, sleepyhead. You hungry? Breakfast is almost ready. I'll make a plate for your sister and have you run it down to her when it's finished."

I couldn't quite say nothin', and then Pop turned to me, still smiling. "Well, go on and wash up, Gabriel. The biscuits be done by the time you finished. Your momma done cooked us up a feast."

"Uh, y-yes sir," I managed, finally. "Thank you, Momma."

But I didn't move. It musta cast some kind of spell on me, seein' them the way they was. Seein' them happy. I didn't wanna look away for fear the spell would break.

"What's got into you, boy?" Pop asked. "You feelin' alright?"

"Y-yes, sir," I stammered. I started to turn to head to the bathroom, but I stopped. I couldn't help myself. "What's going on, anyway? What are ya'll so…happy for?"

I thought I messed up, thought I broke the spell and it was all gonna come falling down around me. But Pop and Momma looked to each other, and Pop nodded. Then Momma turned to me, her face glowin', her eyes shinin'. "Oh, little one, it ain't nothin' short of a miracle. A blessing, one I've been praying so very hard for. Can't you feel it? He still loves us. He's forgiven us." She took a few steps and leaned down in front of me. She tapped my nose with a flour-covered finger. "He's come back to us, Gabriel."

"That's the truth of it, son," Pop said, nodding. "Yes it is. He's come back to us, and now things is gonna be good again 'round here. Just woke up this mornin' and everything felt right as rain. Felt like it used to. Don't it feel good? It's like they was a storm been blowin' right over The Roost these past few weeks." He shook his head. "And then today, the sun finally poked its head out from between them dark clouds and started chasin' them all away." He took a deep breath, came over and put a hand on my shoulder. "Things is gonna be better now, son. Yessir, things is gonna go back to the way they was. Things is gonna be put right. We can finally be a family again."

Some burden, something I ain't even know I'd been hauling around on my back, it just slipped off me then. A lightness came over me, and all the sudden I felt like crying. Laughing and crying all at once. Mikey *had* come back. It hadn't been a dream after all. And we was gonna be a family again. Not separate pieces, broken and scattered, but *whole* again. I wanted to shout with joy, wanted to jump up and down and hug them both until my arms got too weak to hold them. I wasn't about to question it, weren't gonna look a gift horse in the mouth. My face broke out into a smile, and I thought what a funny thing that I still remembered how to do it.

"You've seen him then?" I gushed. My head was all full of sorrys and thank yous and I love yous, and my tongue couldn't wag fast enough to get it all out. I rushed on. "I was so worried last night when I saw him out in the yard. I wanted to tell you, I did. I was all torn up about it. I was just, I was just…I just didn't know what I should do. I thought maybe y'all didn't want him around no more, on account of what happened, you know. I thought maybe you didn't love him." I laughed a little. It felt so good to get it all out. "I love you, Pop. And you, too, Momma! Where is he, anyway? Where's Mikey? Is he out in the barn?"

I looked from Pop to Momma, waiting. I knew immediately that something was wrong.

Very wrong.

Momma's face cracked like a broken mirror. She coughed twice, almost choked, then she took two steps away and held a hand to her mouth. Her hip bumped Pop's coffee cup, and it fell from his hand and spilled across the floor. Pop didn't even notice. His brows furrowed, and his smile broke in half. All the color drained from his face, then a redness began creeping up his neck. His hand on my shoulder tightened.

"What'd you say, son?"

"Ouch, Pop, that hurts," I said. I tried to pry his hand off, but it wouldn't come, the fingers only tightening, nails diggin' into the skin. Pop leaned in closer. His eyes was nearly black.

"Just who in the *hell* did you see last night, boy?"

I ain't wanna say nothin', but them fingers kept digging.

"M-Michael, sir," I breathed out. I looked to the floor, anywhere but at those black eyes. I felt tears running down my cheeks. "It was Michael."

Pop was so close, I could feel his breath steamin' across my face. His mouth opened again, but he ain't say nothin', just ran his tongue over his top teeth. His eyes bore into me, and I waited, waited to feel his open palm across my cheek or his knuckles against my nose. The kitchen had gone blurry. He breathed out, once, twice. Then he gave the slightest nod. I felt the fingers leave my shoulder, and by the time I looked up, he was halfway across the kitchen, reachin' for the shotgun by the back door, callin' to Momma over his shoulder.

"I'll check the garage, Lenore," he yelled out, swingin' the door open. "You and *him* check the basement." And then he was gone.

I looked to Momma, and my heart beat at the bottom of my throat. Gone was any of that brightness, that *lightness*, from before. Gone, too, was the shattered smile. Her face looked like a cake that been pulled out the oven too early...everything all sagging and fallen in on itself. Her eyes were fire.

"*Jesus*, Gabriel," she hissed. No more *little one*.

"Momma, please, I didn't know! Y'all said he came back, th-that, that we was a family again. I thought you knew, I thought—"

"*JESUS*, Gabriel! I was talkin' 'bout *Jesus*! About Jesus comin' back here, back to this house. I've been prayin' so hard since your brother said them sinful things." She wrung her hands together. "And then, your father cast your brother out into the wilderness like God done to Cain after he slain

Abel. I was torn up inside about it…sinner or no, Michael is still my son, my firstborn. But I kept prayin' and prayin', hopin' beyond hope for some kinda answer. And then today, I got it." Her face almost brightened at that. Almost. "Such a lightness this mornin'. Such a…calmness. Jesus was here, Gabriel, and he was happy. And my heart was so full I felt it running out my eyes and ears. I could hardly believe it. And when I saw your daddy, I knew he felt it too."

Jesus. Not Michael.

"Momma, I didn't know, I swear I didn't—"

"*HUSH.*"

Momma turned, paced back to the counter and picked up the cleaver, bits of pink sausage still clinging to the razor-edged blade. She held it out in front of her. Toward me.

Her face shook, and her teeth clenched tightly behind pursed lips. "You hush now! You ruint it, Gabe. I know you didn't know no better, but you did." She cocked her head like she was listenin' for something. "I can't feel him no more." She looked up toward the ceiling, then out toward the dining room, her eyes unfocused. "I can't feel him no more, Gabriel. He's left us again." She shook her head and sighed. The fire was still there in her eyes. "Let's go see if your brother was really so foolish as to come back here. Let's go see if he tempts the wrath of God."

She stalked forward, and I pressed myself back against the wall, turnin' my head sideways, my eyes closed. Maybe I could just melt right through the wallpaper. Maybe she'd just pass me up in her righteous anger. But it weren't no use. She gripped the collar of my night shirt and drug me over to the basement door, shoved me against it. My brain was a fire alarm of noise.

"No, Momma," I tried, takin' just a half step toward the dining room, but she held me in place with her eyes. The hand holdin' the cleaver lifted.

Only a few inches, but it was enough. I faced the door, gripped the knob, and turned. It came open too easily. Like The Roost wanted me to go down there. Down into that darkness.

I went.

I BEEN DOWN these basement stairs a thousand times before. Only a few times since my nightmare of pushin' Momma to her death, though. Only when I had to feed Nat. There weren't no lights on down there now, though, and in that moment, I was certain that these were the same stairs from that awful dream. Certain I was gonna be walkin' forever in that dark. Down, down, down for eternity. Down into the center of the earth. Straight into Hell.

I weren't but a few steps toward that darkness when I realized things wasn't the way they was supposed to be. It was darker than usual, not even the light from Nat's room to break it up, but that weren't what troubled me. It was quiet. Quiet as a grave. You ain't ever have to be all the way in the basement to hear the noise comin' outta Nat's room. She ain't yell too often, but she usually made a little noise down there, singing or laughing or talkin' to herself, readin' her books out loud. But there was none of that. Just like the light that came from her room, the little noises she made was gone, too.

But that weren't the worst thing I noticed. The worst was the smell.

The basement ain't smell right since Pop and Momma set up their little hospital room for Nat. The smell of sickness, of feces, of wet bedding mixed with sweat and of a body being closed up for a while. It was bad, at least at first, but you did get used to it. But now, there was something else, layered in with all those other awful smells. The air was *charged*. It was like when ya digging a hole, the way the dirt smells different the deeper you go. More minerals or something, I guess. Stuff hidden away from the sunshine for too long. I was almost at the bottom step when I remembered where I'd smelled it before. Outside the chicken coop. With Pop Howard, a hatchet in his hand.

It was blood. Lots of blood.

Blood, and that smell from my room.

I couldn't move. Once I realized what exactly I was smellin', my feet refused to go down that last step. My throat closed up, my heart running roughshod in my chest. It felt like a goddam sparrow was stuck in my ribcage, tryin' to beat its way out. The blackness in front of me took on all sorts of shapes. There was something dead down here, lying in a pool of blood right there, right in front of me. And whatever had killed it was still there, too. Hiding in that darkness—waitin' for its next victim. Waitin' for me.

I don't know how long I stood there. Probably just a few moments. But then something nudged the back of my neck. Something cold and metal and smelling of butchered meat.

"*Move*," Momma hissed in my ear.

So I moved.

That first step was like walkin' off a cliff. My feet were anvils, my legs stuck in wet cement. My bare toes were curled, waitin' to kick against a cold body, to step into something warm and wet and sticky. I shuffled forward in that darkness, a blind man walkin' across a shootin' gallery. The basement was big, but now it was a warehouse. I heard someone cryin', the whimpers echoing off the walls. It took me a moment to realize that the sound was coming from me. New tears stung my eyes, but it ain't make no difference in that inky blackness.

My feet never left the floor, just drug along through the dirt and dust. I was about halfway across the room when something brushed across my forehead. A spider, all its hairy legs running across my face. A centipede burrowing itself into my hair. I screamed then, and stopped, and Momma bumped into the back of me, that cold steel hitting my neck again. I brushed at my head, not wanting to touch the thing but just wanting it off me. My fingers felt something thin, a small, hard thing at the end. I breathed out. The pull-string. It was the goddam pull-string for the bare lightbulb hanging from the ceiling. I closed my eyes tight. I pulled it.

Light flooded the room. My eyes flew open, ready for the bloodbath. But the room was empty.

Not completely empty. There were the old wooden crates stacked into the corner, the laundry piled up by the copper wash pot and the mangler, the workbench with a half-dozen of Pop's unfinished projects. But there was no blood on the floor. No dead things. I looked around in a panic. The door to the canning room was tucked away in the corner, slightly ajar. Nat's room now.

"D-don't see him, M-momma. H-he ain't here."

Momma ain't say nothin'. The cleaver against my shoulder did the talkin' for her. It nudged me forward, toward the back corner of the basement. Toward that door.

The smell was stronger there. And if the door was open, how come the lights was off? How come I couldn't hear nothin'? I stopped at the threshold. I thought of Michael, creepin' through the yard, somethin' in his hand. Had it been a knife? No, he wouldn't hurt Nat. He wasn't so angry that he would do that. Would he?

The single light in the middle of the basement couldn't hardly reach here, and beyond the open door was just darkness. Silence. I leaned in just the slightest. Was there a noise then? A single step crunching on the dirt floor? A sigh?

"Natalie?" I almost whispered. "Natalie, you in there?"

Of course she was, right? Where else could she be? Poor thing could hardly even sit up in bed without causing herself a whole mess of pain. She couldn't leave that room, let alone climb the basement stairs. But where was she? Why wasn't she answering?

Sleepin', I thought. *Only sleepin'*.

"Natalie?" I tried again, as I pushed open the door.

It creaked on its worn hinges like a wounded animal. The meager light from the basement fell across a corner of the floor inside the old canning room. My legs lost all feeling.

The light shone on a pool of blood on the dirty cement, as black as midnight and thick as syrup. It stretched from the doorjamb to the far wall, all the way to the body slumped there.

Michael. And dead, too. All the color of the living drained from his face, head lying crooked cross his slumped shoulders. His neck shone pale in that weak light. The wound there ran nearly ear to collarbone. It weren't no blade that done it, neither. There was…pieces of him missing. Chunks of flesh just…just gone. Coyotes, that's what I thought first. A coyote had gotten into the yard one night, found its way into the goat pen. That's how Michael looked now, like one of them goats, like some wild animal had caught his scent and needed to feed. Like something had dug its teeth in and shook their head until the skin and muscle and ligaments all tore loose. Ravaged. My own guts boiled. Blood still bubbled outta the wound, and he had one dirty hand up near it, the fingers clenched into a claw. His other hand lay at his side in the pooling blood. A silver flask was lying beside it, covered in red. The thing I'd seen last night from my window.

My head turned away from my brother. Toward the rest of the room. Not wanting to see, but having to all the same.

The bed was empty.

I fell backward. Couldn't help it. I staggered against the open door, and then bile rose in my throat, and my raging guts emptied themselves on the floor, thick runners of spit and vomit mixing with the blood there, the pool inside the room finding an escape into the basement now that the door was all the way open. My head was a kaleidoscope of horror, a spinning Ferris wheel, a carousel of whirling lights and devilish dreams, spinnin' and spinnin', all red, all stinking, and my feet weren't on the floor but somewhere floating out in space, my body somewhere far down below me. I could hear Momma behind me, prayin' and cryin', all *Dear Jesus Oh Lord Please Help Us*. My guts emptied again, and then I was gagging, choking, my insides feeling like they was bleeding too. My throat was dry, and every breath tore open the soft skin inside, but I couldn't stop. I fell to my knees, couldn't figure out how to work my legs, how to hold myself up no more. Some instinct kicked in then, some wild animal sense deep inside me, and then I was crawling through the blood and the vomit, backing out across the basement floor, not thinkin', not feelin', just needin' to get away away from the blood, from that room.

Fingers gripped the nape of my neck. Held me in place. It was Michael, back from the dead. *Come little brother, come see. Come see what happens when you're cast out into the wilderness.*

But it was Momma.

"Get up, Gabriel."

Somehow, I got up.

I looked to Momma, and I regretted it immediately. Momma was gone. Ain't nothin' but stone and petrified wood and two eyes as black as coal dust starin' back at me. The cleaver came up, and this time it weren't angled to prod, but angled to do what it was made for. To cut. To cleave. To sever. I knew what it was tellin' me. I knew where it wanted me to go.

I lurched forward, toward that yawning door. Toward that room of death. I couldn't hardly see through the tears, but I ain't need to see to know where to put my hand to find the pull-string. I clasped it with numb fingers, and I pulled and waited.

And there was Natalie. She looked smaller, somehow, though I'd just seen her yesterday when I brought her a plate. Skinnier. She was standin' in the corner, hunched over a bit, her back to the door, her nose nearly touching the wall. Her golden hair hung dirty and matted. I could see the blood even from behind. It trailed down the side of her neck and over her gown, most of it already dried to a burnt brown. Her hands, her small, delicate hands, were at her side, covered in it— her fingers black, nails crusted over.

She turned her head slowly, not much, just enough so I could see one eye. One pale blue eye, the pupil as flat as the head of a tack, the whites spiderwebbed with veins. Mold like tar grew in the corners. Her lips were blue. They parted slightly, revealin' just a smudge of teeth. They were stained with blood. Little pieces of meat stuck out between them.

"He wanted me to leave, Gabey," Natalie whispered, still not lookin' at me all the way. "He wanted me to leave y'all behind and run away with him. He was gonna lift me up and take me away from here, and I, I couldn't let him do that, could I? I couldn't." She shook her head. "I'm not supposed to leave here, am I, Gabey? I'm not allowed."

A single black tear dripped from her eye; a single shining track running through the drying gore on her cheek.

And then she turned.

And that's when I knew. Knew for sure what I had only guessed at when I saw that one eye.

It weren't the eyes of my sister staring back at me.

It was the eyes of the man on the pond.

Flat. Dead. Angry.

She took a step forward.

"Natalie?" I choked out, but it sounded more like a cry. Fresh tears streamed down my face. "Natalie, please. No."

She took another step. I raised my hands out in front of me.

"P-please."

She spoke. Her voice was dry and old now—ancient.

"You wouldn't want to try to make me leave, would ya, Gabey?"

Another step.

"N-no, Nat! No. N-never, uh…y-you can stay here. You can stay here just as long as you like."

"I *have* to stay here. For *Him*, Gabriel. You know that, right? You understand, don't ya?"

The tears were comin' faster now, and my throat was all closed up. I pursed my lips, tried to keep the cries inside, but they broke through. All I could do was nod.

She took another step. Only a couple feet away now.

A part of me wanted to back up. To run. To lash out. But a powerful tiredness was singing through my bones, through my head, through my whole life. I was so goddam tired of running, of fighting. I just wanted it to be over. All of it. End the nightmare. Finally rest.

"You can help me, Gabriel," she cooed in her cracked voice. "Michael thought he was helpin', but he wasn't. He was tryin' to leave. But *you* can help. It's almost over now. You want it to be over, don't ya? I can't do it myself, you know. Will you help, Gabriel? Will you help your little sister?"

She reached a hand out, and still, I didn't move. *Couldn't* move. I let her small fingers grip my wrist, and her skin was cold and her grip strong, and it made me feel weak all over. But my legs ain't buckle, even as much as they was shakin'. I let her grip my wrist, and I cried and I cried but I ain't pull back, and I ain't run. I stayed. I stayed there for Natalie, and this seemed to make her happy. She flashed me another bloody grin. Her black pupils pulsed in the light.

She took another step forward. The last step. Now, she was right in front of me, and I could smell that same smell from my bedroom. From all those sleepless nights. Desiccated fruit and moldering wood. The coppery tang of blood and death. There was a wildness to it that sent shivers runnin' through me. Her hand tightened on my wrist. I looked her straight in the eye.

"Please."

It was just a prayer, a small one, but to God or the devil or to Mr. Trench, I don't know.

She shook her head softly. Her eyes stayed flat, but she bit her lower lip. Coulda been sympathy, or disappointment, or remorse, but I couldn't tell. She opened her mouth again, and this time it weren't to give me no smile. I could see all her teeth. Some of them still baby teeth. Her mouth opened, and her eyes closed, and she leaned forward. I closed my eyes too, ready to feel the bite of those baby teeth on my throat.

A wrecking ball slammed into my side. I flew across the room. I felt my jaw click, and then my left hand met the wall, and I heard the sound of tiny bones snapping. The pain hit me right away, little fireworks of heat rushing up my arm. I cried out, slid down the wall, slipping on the mess on the floor to rest beside Mikey.

Momma was standin' in the small room right where I'd been standin' just a moment before, burnin' immaculate like Christ himself risen from the tomb, the cleaver held out in front of her like some kinda magic talisman. She was shakin' from head to toe, everything vibratin'. A bit of that stoniness from before had left her face, and I could see Momma in there again, a little crazy, a little confused, righteously pissed-off. But it was all *Momma*. She looked from her youngest baby standin' before her with blood ringin' her mouth, down to her oldest baby all bled out and discarded on the floor in the dirt at her feet. She shook the blade at Natalie.

"You demon," she spit out. "You devil. Y'had your brother fooled, didn't ya? Had us all fooled. I shoulda seen it, shoulda seen you for what you was. You been touched since the day I brought you into this world, marked with original sin we could never hope to worsh off. I shoulda listened to my sister, shoulda had you sent away when you pushed me down them stairs. Always talkin' that nonsense…speaking in tongues to the father of lies. Speakin' that snake talk. Oh, Lord forgive me, but I was blinded by love. But the scales have been lifted from my eyes, and I see what His light is showin' me now, demon. I see the blackness in your spirit. There's a malady on this family, on this house, and you're the cause of it. And if we're meant to keep our everlasting souls intact, then you must be cut from us like rot must be cut from an infected wound."

Momma raised that cleaver, raised it up high. Natalie watched it go. She ain't never move to stop it, never even lifted her hands up to defend herself. She was resigned to her fate, same as I'd been. But something changed in her. As that blade came sweeping down, I saw the change come over her. The blackness receded in her eyes, the flat pupils shrinking, the scowl dropping from her face. It was like watching somebody getting' hit with a pail of cold water. The change hit her in an instant, and then she was just a little girl again, as scared and as helpless as I felt. Lost and hurt. Just little Natalie again. I was movin' before I knew I'd had the thought.

"Momma, no!" I screamed, and then I was barreling into her hip, my good hand punching out to hit the wrist of the hand holdin' the cleaver. It fell down onto the floor. Momma gasped, the wind knocked from her, and she reached out, grabbed me around the shoulders, embraced me like she hadn't done for a long, long time, back when I needed her comfort, back when she still had some to give, before the world had gone crazy. She held me, and we fell to the floor, mother and son, together. Together, one last time.

Natalie was over us in an instant. The light from the single bulb ringed her head. The cleaver shone brightly in her hand. Her eyes was black. She didn't hesitate.

The blade came flashin' down as fast a guillotine. I rolled off of Momma, tryin' to get away, but I felt fire in my shoulder as that metal kissed my skin. I screamed. I rolled over onto Mikey's legs, my body all twisted up. The sound of metal hittin' flesh and bone rang out in the small room, and it sounded like there were a thousand cleavers comin' down, rainin' down over and over. Momma was screamin' now, too, no more righteous fury, and I covered my head, screamed right along with her. Natalie grunted with every fall of that blade.

THWACK THWACK THWACK

Something crawled across my leg and fixed there on my ankle. I tried to shake it off. I glanced down. It was Momma's hand, holding me tight. Holdin' on for dear life. Her eyes found me, pinned me there, and I watched as her screams got weaker and weaker. It made me even sicker to see her hand on me. I wanted to help, didn't want to watch her go, but it was like a drowning person grabbin' on to someone who barely had they head above the water. I could feel every cut of that cleaver through her hand, felt the vibration of every bone breakin' right through the floor. I had to look away. I glanced up, straight into Mikey's pale, dead face. A piece of my mind broke away then.

That'll be me, soon.

I ain't never leavin' this place.

This is what's it's like to die.

The violence behind me, all around me, it was still climbing, but underneath it there was thunder. Mortar fire heard from the depths of a foxhole. And just when I ain't think the old house could take anymore noise, that this whole world was right on the edge of exploding, I recognized that thunder for what it was: someone was runnin' down the basement stairs.

Pop bull rushed into the small room, and hell itself came with him. Shotgun clutched in one hand, one big size-12 shit-kickin' boot already raised. That boot sunk into Natalie's nose as she straddled what was left of our Momma. I heard the crack of cartilage, saw that small nub of flesh collapse under the weight of Pop's fury as she fell. Her head snapped back so fast I was sure her spine was broke, but she was already tryin' to sit back up with a long, keening wail escaping from her throat. It was an awful sound, maybe even more awful than that blade sinkin' into meat— rage and grief and hopelessness all mixed up together. I ain't have it in me to scream anymore, or to cry. Nat's neck wasn't broke, but something inside her sure was. Her lungs was full of roofin' nails and river mud. Pop never looked down at his wife, or at his two kids lyin' there in blood. He only had eyes for Natalie.

He reached out and took a fistful of her hair in his free hand.

"You want her so bad?" he said. "You want her so bad, then I'll bring her to ya, ya bastard."

I thought he was talkin' to Natalie, talkin' 'bout Momma lyin' right there at his feet, her insides all hangin' out now. But he took that fistful of hair and pulled hard, neck muscles strainin', and then he was draggin' Nat through the mess on the floor and on out the door to the basement without so much as a single glance around the room. Little Nat kicked a bit, her hands clawin' at his grip on her head, but it seemed like most the fight had gone outta her.

Pop drug her behind him as he crossed the floor and started up the steps. I watched 'em for a moment, not wanting to follow, but wantin' to stay there in the blood of my mother and brother even less.

I staggered to my feet, cradlin' my busted wrist in my other hand. Blood was pourin' from the wound on my shoulder, that fiery kiss of the cleaver, and I'd been cryin' so long and so hard my head felt like it were full of hornets, but I lurched forward on legs made of wood. When I got to them basement stairs, I heard the outside door bang shut above me.

It had been hard walkin' down them stairs toward that liquid dark, but walkin' up 'em was even harder. A trail of blood ran from the top of the stairs to the kitchen door that led to the backyard, and I followed it. The sunlight felt like a thousand needles pokin' into my eyes. I blinked away the pain and the tears as best as I could. They were right where I knew they'd be, right out there in the water. The shotgun had been cast aside in the mud around the pond, and Pop was halfway toward the center of it, still draggin' Natalie behind him, the green water turnin' black in her wake where it rinsed the blood and gore from her face, her hair, and her gown.

"Here she is!" Pop was screamin'. Dark stains were spreadin' on his work shirt under his arms and down the middle of his back. "She's right here. Come and take what's left of her. You hear me, Trench? I'm bringin' her right to ya!"

The water rose from his calves to his knees then to his waist. He stopped when he reached the middle. He lifted Natalie up by the hair, and she cried out, weakly. She tried to cough out some words, maybe just his name, but Pop gripped her neck with his other hand. I knew Pop's strength, had seen him wrestle many a stubborn mule into submission, and I knew one squeeze and Nat's neck woulda snapped in two. But he ain't do that. He just held her there. I watched from the shore. I'd become a ghost again, just a spectator in my own life. A witness. Pop stared down into Natalie's eyes, and there was tears runnin' down over his stubbled cheeks, fallin' into the water. He stared for what seemed like a long time. He shook his head, and the pressure of his fingers on Nat's throat let up just a bit.

"Daddy."

It was a soft as a sound could be. A dandelion seed floatin' on the breeze and landin' on a blade of grass. So fragile, it seemed as if I thought too hard about it, that it would split into a hundred smaller sounds and cease to exist. But it was there. Natalie, from somewhere deep within the wreckage of her broken body. Still there, somewhere. Pop's shoulders sagged at the sound of it, and more tears came drippin' off his face. He brought her close, took the hand from her throat and put it under her, supportin' her. He let go of that fistful of hair. He ran a calloused finger down her cheek. He spoke just above a whisper, but the day was calm, and the water carried the sound over to me on the shore.

"Ain't your fault, little one. You was born into this. You was born into this, as innocent as a lamb." He sighed. "And only death can save ya from it."

"Daddy," she choked out again, and this time a little blood came out with the word.

If Pop heard her, I don't know. He gripped her shoulders, and he shoved her head underwater.

"This what you want?" he screamed, his voice crackin'. "This time gonna pay for all?"

The tendons on his neck stood out taut as tripwires as he held her there, held his only daughter, his baby girl, under that green water. His arms shook with the effort of it. Small, pale hands came up from that water, clawin' at him, beatin' at him. But he held her there like a fevered preacher givin' an unholy baptism, tryin' to drown all the sins of a lifetime, tryin' to kill whatever demons were inside her. Eventually, the small hands fell away. Pop wasn't shoutin' words no more, just screamin' like he was bein' lashed with a dozen bullwhips, screamin' and cryin'. Standing on the shore, I was screamin' now, too.

I fell to my knees in the mud. It was like my body done gave up right there on the shore. Everything hurt inside me, everything was wrong. Everything hollow, my insides all scooped out. I was like a shed snakeskin. I slumped over, my head hittin' my knees. My ears was poundin', the blood rushin' so hard through me, and a blackness started to wash over everything around me. I held my hand out to the side, tryin' to keep from fallin' over, and my fingers brushed something cool and smooth in the mud beside me.

It was too big for me, really, even if I had full use of both my hands and my shoulder ain't have a chunk of meat gouged outta it. But I picked it up anyway, held it out best as I could. I aimed that shotgun out to where Pop was drownin' Natalie. It needed to be over. All of it. I ain't even call out to Daddy. My lungs was too weak. But he musta known something, cause he turned right as the whole world exploded in front of me.

The recoil slammed the stock of the gun into my chest, crackin' three of my ribs all in one fell swoop. The pellets splattered the water around where Pop stood, almost looked like it was rainin'. But some of them musta found Daddy, cause he started fallin', his grip loosening, and then I was fallin' too, the last of whatever will I had left leakin' out of me. Everything started to go black, and this time I couldn't fight it, just let it take me as I fell into the mud. Right before I landed, I saw someone else out there in the water with my daddy and my sister. A man, standing just above 'em. A man with long, white hair and puckered, red eyes. He was smiling. And then I hit the ground and everything was gone.

CHAPTER TEN

I was nine years old when our house burnt down. Dad and I had been living there together for about two years, ever since he and my mom had split up. Well, ever since she disappeared one night. It wasn't much, just a single-story two-bedroom house nestled in a neighborhood of a couple dozen other houses just like it, but it was home. The fire had started two houses over from ours, but it had been a dry summer, and the wind was blowing just south of hurricane speeds. The small little city lots meant there wasn't much more than a dozen feet of space between buildings. The fire spread like gasoline had been poured on the whole block. Dad yanked me from my bed sometime in the night, and the smoke was already so bad I couldn't see down the hallway to the front door. We had to crawl. When we got to the road, our little section of the city was in complete chaos. Firetrucks and ambulances, neighbors carrying what they could of their lives strapped to their backs and held against their chests. Smoke and flames and crying children and flashing lights tore the night in two. Our car was stuck in the garage, and the garage had been the first part of our house to catch fire, so we walked down the street and sat against the curb and watched as our house and a handful of others burned. Three firetrucks fought the blaze, but it still took them five hours to get it under control. Even so, they barely kept the maelstrom contained. They may not have saved the whole city that night, but it damn sure felt like it. I watched the firemen afterwards. Sweat poured down their soot-covered faces, exhaustion carved into their features. They sat against trees or the trucks or on the curbs like us, eyes focused on some faraway place, drinking water. They didn't talk or laugh. The fire had burned that out of them.

And that's what I saw when I looked at Uncle Pete sitting there beside me. A man burned out, not by fire, but by the past. Completely spent. There was exhaustion etched beneath his eyes and in the way his shoulders seemed to sag, but there was pain there, too. It was hurting him to dredge these old things up and examine them. To hold them in his hands and turn them over again and again. I wondered how many times he had looked at them over the years. I guessed not many. Even at 26, I knew there were some things in life you had to box up and put away on a shelf in the back of a closet in your mind. Somewhere you wouldn't ever come upon it by accident, a hidden place you could only go because you wanted to. It was safer that way. And really, it was the only way you could survive some things. The only way to stay sane.

I had boxed up this entire place—The Roost and the pond and even Uncle Pete—the day my father killed himself. I'd kept it in the back of a closet of my own. And although I didn't take it down and open it up very often these days, the box never got a chance to collect dust. Even so, being back at The Roost, sitting in front of the spot where my father spent the last moments of his life was damn near killing me. I looked at Pete again and my heart squeezed painfully at the grief I saw there. Christ, what was all this doing to him? He hadn't just lost a brother out here, but a father and a grandfather and an aunt as well. And why the pond? What evil thing had taken root in its olive-green depths? I looked to its edge just a few feet from where I sat, and I pulled my feet back and tucked them under my chair.

The water had gone down quite a bit now, at least a couple of feet, and it was as if the skin of a giant had been peeled back to reveal the bones beneath.

The shoreline had grown. It was obscene, somehow, seeing it that way—seeing it stripped and naked. The spongey bottom glowed electric green, with bits of brown and gray poking through like rotting teeth from diseased gums. Piles of decaying leaves like tiny burial mounds littered the bottom. Broken sticks and rocks and a few flattened beer cans. I wasn't surprised to see there were bones there, too. Little bones. Tiny skeletons. It was hard to tell what they were from. Birds, I think, but some were larger. Racoons, maybe, or opossums. Squirrels and groundhogs. They lay on the bottom like miniature shipwrecks. I looked out to the center of the pond, to the deepest part, and I wondered what treasure lay there. A chill danced down my spine at the thought of it. I wasn't sure I wanted to find out.

"Christ, Uncle Pete," I said, not wanting to talk, but needing to break the awful silence. "I never knew any of that. I'm so—"

"Gotta check the hose," Uncle Pete blurted out, cutting me off. He sat up quickly—perhaps a bit too quickly—and he tottered on his feet for a moment. He stared down at the mud in front of us. Probably picturing his dad there, his dad as a little kid, holding a gun that was half as tall as he was.

"You need help?" I offered.

Pete raised his head, and his eyes found mine. There weren't tears there, but I wish there were. Instead, they were just blank and glassy. The eyes of a stuffed and mounted deer head. He shook his head.

"Naw, I…I can handle it. Thanks, Marcus."

As he shuffled off toward the Honey River, I stood up to stretch my legs. I tried to shake the feeling there was more to all this, something more that Uncle Pete was holding back from me. I frowned up at the sky. A blanket of steel wool hung above us, dark pockets of deeper black nestled in its coils. No rain, yet, thank God, but it couldn't be far off. The air felt pregnant with it. I wandered in the opposite direction of the Honey, not wanting to disturb

Uncle Pete. I had my own things to worry about, anyway. My own secrets.

Like my Great-Aunt Natalie whispering in my ear.

He's lying, he's lying.

It's so dark down here, Marcus.

Was Uncle Pete lying? And if so, lying about *what*?

No, don't do it, asshole. Don't put those fucking walls up again. You have to let someone in eventually. You have to learn to trust again. My head was heavy as I walked. It was Tera I thought of first, but Uncle Pete was right there, too. Poor Uncle Pete, alone out here all these years. Living with all these ghosts. How long had it been since he'd been able to confide in anyone? Wasn't he putting his trust in me, telling me all of this? The day was turning out to be heavier than I expected, and I was thankful for the few moments alone to get my head straight. Besides, my bladder was filled to capacity, all those beers begging to be let out. The wind kicked up a beat as I neared the cornfields; the drying leaves whispered in a chorus. *He's back. He's home. He's here.* But this place wasn't anyone's home, certainly not mine. I unzipped my pants and let the corn know what I thought of their declarations.

When I got back, Uncle Pete stood at the edge of the declining shoreline. He had a fresh beer in his hand. The old guy could really pack them away, but he didn't appear to be drunk. In college, I had a friend named Dustin Browning who had crippling social anxiety. He hardly ever left his dorm room, preferring the comfort of online games or movies to the fear-inducing possibility of real-world interactions. There were occasions where I could persuade him to join me at a bar or at a party, as long as the party wasn't too crowded. And, as long as he could have a few drinks before we left. He called those drinks his *Courage Juice*, and I bet Uncle Pete was thinking the same thing about all those beers. You can't have courage unless you're afraid, and Pete looked like a man on the edge of some terrible abyss, a soldier getting ready to rush out of his foxhole and charge across enemy lines. I wondered, not for the first time, if he should be doing all this, if his old heart could handle it. But that wasn't my place. Before today, I didn't know a damn thing about the horrors he'd already faced in his life. He was a tough old bastard. I was thankful I was finally getting to know him.

He saw me coming back and nodded to me.

"Hose look alright?" I asked.

"Yep, she's running slick as shit. Shouldn't be but a couple more hours and we'll have this sunavabitch drained to the bottom."

I sat back down in my lawn chair. "What then?"

He shrugged and settled back into his own chair. "Guess we'll find out. Mayhap we can finally lay these ghosts to rest."

I guess that's what we'd been doing this whole time. Letting our ghosts haunt us just one more time before they finally got some peace. I checked my phone. Nearly two in the afternoon already. No new messages, of course. I put it into airplane mode and slid it back into my pocket. This was almost over, and I wanted to be here, really *here*, for the whole thing.

I was bursting with questions, so many thoughts swirling around in my head, but I didn't want to push. This was Uncle Pete's story to tell, after all. Still, I felt my throat loosening up and filling with a dozen words, but before I could say anything, Pete cleared his throat and spoke first.

"He didn't die, ya know. Pop Howard. A few of those pellets got him, but that old gun proved to be just a little too much for Daddy to handle. Most of the shot sprayed into the water. I bet when we get to the bottom, we find a handful of 'em still stuck in the mud.

"The milkman came by not too long after. Darby Milliron was his name, worked over at the Shelby Dairy. When he talked to the papers, he said he came down here and dropped off his delivery…was just about to leave when he heard some odd things coming from the back of the house. He came 'round the corner and saw Daddy slumped on the shore of the pond, his shirt soaked in blood, the shotgun laying at his side. Natalie was floating in the middle of the water. He said he could tell right off she was a goner, and he thought the same for Daddy too, until he heard him moanin'. Pop Howard was in a frenzy. He was covered in blood, too. He had a steel bucket in his hands, and he was dipping it in the pond and chucking the water off to the side like a man trying to save a sinking ship. He didn't even notice Darby. Darby wasn't the sharpest tool in the shed, but he knew when things wasn't right. And there was nothin' about what was goin' on back there that was right. He turned tail and huffed it back to Hilborn. When the Sheriff finally got out there, Pop still had that pail in his hands, still tossin' that water away. Ain't even say a word when they cuffed him and put him in the back of the cruiser.

"Daddy had a rough go of it. He woke up when the ambulance got there, and he got to see them pull his baby sister from the water. Her eyes was wide open, but she was well past seeing anything. She looked like a car whose headlights stayed on after the motor gave out. He passed back out at the sight of it. When he woke again, he was in the hospital…had to stay there for a few weeks. Couldn't eat much, couldn't hardly sleep. When he slept, he screamed, and when he was awake, he cried. The police questioned him a few times, but he was all wrung out. His whole family gone in one day…Christ, Marcus, I don't know how he made it, I really don't. He turned fourteen in that hospital bed before they finally let him go.

"He didn't have no family left, not really. A few cousins on Lenore's side, but they lived out in Minnesota and had never even met him. The state took him in, and he bounced around the foster system for a few years. Those were hard times, too, and I don't want to think about what he went through. Somehow, he held himself together though. Graduated high school and everything. That's where he met Momma, his junior year at Shelby High School. Found a bit of love in between all the heartbreak, God bless him.

"Now, I know you're probably wondering what came of Pop Howard. The state wanted to pin all three deaths on him...it was too messy of a thing, too *scandalous*. And Pop didn't do himself no favors. He was a broken man. He didn't try to defend himself. Maybe the thought of tellin' them how it had all happened felt a bit like spittin' on the graves of his wife and his daughter and his son, or maybe he didn't want to give the town more rumors to spread around. Regardless, he wouldn't say a word in his defense, not even to his court-appointed lawyer. But Daddy did. In between all those waking nightmares in the hospital, he gave a full account of everything that had been going on in the house. Everything but Mr. Trench. Even at thirteen, even after walking through Hell and comin' out the other side, he knew there were some things that just couldn't be said out loud. Not if he wanted them to believe everything else, that is. Even though it sounded like a tall tale, the state was forced to believe him; the evidence all backed up his story. Natalie's hand had blisters from where she held the cleaver, and in her mouth, stuck in her teeth, was...well, you get it. The trial was a short one; Pop's lawyer managed to get the murder charge lowered to manslaughter, the best he could do without any help from his client. Still, Pop got ten years. Never said a word in court. Never even gave a reaction when the guilty verdict came down, just lowered his head and allowed the bailiff to take him away without any fight. Daddy didn't show up, though he could have. He never got to say goodbye to his old man.

"Daddy didn't hear from Pop for three years. Not a single letter. No phone calls. He could've, you know, could've found out where Daddy was livin'. He moved around between a few different families, but they was all within twenty miles of Hilborn. And Pop Howard was just over in Mansfield at the Ohio State Reformatory. There weren't a no contact order or nothin'.

But Pop was silent for those three years, and Daddy was silent, too. And then, right around the time Daddy turned eighteen, a letter came. It was from Pop; Daddy recognized the writin' on the envelope straight off. It was short, too, despite the years since they'd talked:

Gabriel,

You a man now, and I think it's time we had ourselves a talk. Come see me. There's things you need to know.

Pop

"So, that's how, at eighteen, Daddy found himself inside the old prison, sittin' at a table in a room made of concrete with no windows, with Pop sittin' across from him. Pop looked genuinely happy to see him. Prison hadn't been kind to him…the slab muscle he'd built up from years of farm work had turned soft, and there were bags under his eyes as big as hay bales. He looked frail to Daddy, no longer the ragin' demon of his youth but an old man now. But the old man's eyes still glimmered when he saw his only child, one little spark of life left in him. Normal visitation at that time was supposed to be only one hour, but Pop's lawyer pulled a few strings, seeing as how it had been so long since the two seen't each other. They talked for over four hours. Daddy didn't know it at the time, but it was the last time he would see Pop Howard." Uncle Pete rubbed his hands together, the arthritic knuckles popping. "The very next morning, the guards opened up his cell to find him hanging from a bedsheet."

Uncle Pete sat forward, fumbled another smoke out the pack in his shirt pocket. He didn't bother offering me one this time, and for that, I was thankful. I wasn't sure I had the willpower to say no. He took a drag and held it in for a moment, lost in thought. When he spoke, his words came out riding a wave of smoke.

"He didn't leave a note, if you're wondering, and I guess he didn't need to, neither. What happened out here was more a reason than any words could ever say."

CHAPTER ELEVEN

"When me and Jim was little, we had the run of this place. Same as you when you was a little'n, Marcus. Everywhere but the pond and the basement, right?" Pete let out a thin laugh. "Only difference is, it was easy to keep ya away from those places. You was a good kid…and since you was a guest those times when you was here, you minded me and your aunt when we told ya these things." He waved his hand. "And no bother about you and Laurie in the kitchen with the basement door. Yes, she told me all about it. That only proves my point, that you was a good kid. She caught ya before there was any damage done, and you never tried to get down there again. But it was different for ya daddy and me. We lived here. The pond and the basement…they was part of our home. Part of our day to day. And everybody knows, you want a kid to do something, well, you just tell him he ain't allowed. Everybody knows that. Daddy did, too. Having to grow up so quick didn't make him forget what it was like to be a child.

"I wasn't but eight or nine, which means ya dad was ten or eleven, when Grandpa Gabe sat us down and talked to us about The Roost. About what had happened here. It…it weren't an easy thing to hear. And he didn't spare our little minds. We heard about everything. Every bite, every cut, every gunshot. Mayhap it was a bit harsh, but Daddy weren't much older than us when he lived it. It was important to him that we knew, that when he said we wasn't s'posed to play down in the basement or sneak off and go swimming in the pond, that he had a good reason for it. It worked. He was a hard man, and he could come down on us like a sack of bricks when we done something wrong, but he never had to tell us again. He also made us promise him something."

Pete took off his hat and wiped at his brow. He cocked an eye at me. There was no judgement in his gaze, but something close to it. An appraisal of sorts. He put his hat back on. "Yes, I know, I know," he mumbled, taking a sip of his beer. "I'm goin' to. Came this far didn't I?" He cast an eye over to me, but I feigned like I hadn't heard anything.

"Ya grandpa made me and ya dad promise we'd never have kids of our own. And, if we did, we would never bring 'em here to The Roost. He said it weren't a safe place for kids." Pete shook his head. "And I know you're wonderin' why he had me and Jim if he was so concerned for our safety. Why he would bring young ones into this world, why he would raise 'em up right here where the worst things imaginable had happened in his life. Truth is, I don't know, and I ain't sure he did neither. I don't think people know half the reasons they do things. For him, I think part of it was loneliness. He grew up with a family and a full house, and by the time he got back here, by the time he'd become a man and had a wife and wanted to settle down and start a life for himself, well, he didn't have no family no more. He was alone, side for Momma. I think by havin' us he thought he could fill that hole in him, that he could change his history a bit. That by raising up his own family in this house, he could prove that there weren't no curse, no old evil in the ground here, that the Castle family name didn't have to always end in tragedy. He was wrong. By the time he set us down and told us his story, he knew it himself."

"Asshole," I blurted out. I didn't know I was going to; it just came out.

"What's that?" Uncle Pete asked. But he knew.

I sighed, and I felt it roll down my shoulders. "Dad," I said. "What a fucking asshole. So, he knew all this? He knew everything that had happened out here, but he never thought it'd be a good idea to share any of it with his only son? I don't get it, man, I just…I just don't understand." My vision blurred, and I shut my eyes, trying to force the tears to go backwards. "He was all I had. And I was all *he* had. Growing up, it was always just me and him. Mom wasn't around…yeah, she called on my birthday every year. At least until she didn't. Took me clothes shopping before the school year started a few times. But it was just me and Dad. I thought…I guess I thought we were a lot closer than that. I thought he trusted me. I guess he really thought I was just too stupid to understand. Too fragile, or something. Too immature."

I emptied my beer can in two great guzzles, then I crushed it in my hand. I considered throwing it in the middle of pond for a moment, like it was some big act of defiance, like somehow it would make me feel better. Like it would assuage some of the pain building up inside of me. Might as well go find a door to slam, I thought, or just stand up and stomp my feet. Instead of any of those things, I laughed, but it came out closer to a cry. My eyes swam over to the cooler. *That's* what I needed. Getting another beer would make me feel better, not throwing the can like some little child.

"You need another?" I asked, as I fished around in the rapidly emptying cooler.

"Think I'm doing okay, Marcus," Uncle Pete said, and after a moment of hesitation, "I ain't in no position to give advice, but maybe after that one you should be okay, too. At least, for a little while."

The anger in me flashed again, but there wasn't much behind it, just a lit fuse without the stick of dynamite. I nodded, felt my wet cheeks get warm with embarrassment.

"Yeah, I think you're right. I guess they're hitting me a little harder than I thought."

"Nah, it ain't that," Pete said. He waved his beer around, gesturing at the fields and the river and everything in between. "It's all this, Marcus. It's all this…all this *history*. You stay here long enough it starts seeping into you, the same way toxic chemicals can seep into the groundwater."

"You seem to be doing alright," I said with a laugh—a *real* laugh this time. "I did four years at Bowling Green, and even with all the frat parties and keggers and dollar shot nights at the hole-in-the-wall bars, I don't think I met anyone who could pack it away like you, Uncle Pete. Not without being piss-drunk and cross-eyed, that is."

Uncle Pete laughed at that. He leaned back and chugged the rest of his beer, crushing the can like I had. Then he tossed it out into the middle of the pond. Of course, he did. He patted his belly and let out a burp.

"Well, they say practice makes perfect, don't they? I'm retired, Marcus. I've had lots of time to practice doin' nothing." He started laughing, and then I joined in, and pretty soon, we could hardly stop. Maybe it was just all the nasty things we'd been ruminating on, or maybe it was just all that anxiety and stress and anger finally finding an escape hatch, but whatever it was, it felt good, and neither of us stopped until our stomachs hurt and the tears running down our face were the happy kind. When we had finally caught our breath, Uncle Pete leaned over and put his oven-mitt of a hand on my shoulder.

"I love you, Marcus. I hope you know that. Always have."

My hand reached up and found his. "I love you, too, Uncle Pete."

"Me and ya Aunt Laurie always did love you…loved having you around here. Lotta bad memories in The Roost, but you was never part of 'em. You were part of the good ones…the slice of sunshine battin' away the acres of storm clouds. Just about gutted us when you and ya daddy stopped comin' around."

That took a little bit of the sugar out of my coffee. I felt the smile wilt on my face.

"Yeah," I said, "that gutted me, too. This place was…well, you know, after our place burnt down over in Ashland, Dad and I never really found our footing again. I mean, we had other houses we lived in. Some for a lot longer than the two years we spent over there. But none really felt like home as much as that one did, and, it always felt like we were—was— drifting a bit after that. Like we'd been out to sea for too long, and when we got back to the shore everything was still moving around us, even though we were staying in the same place. Does that make sense?" Uncle Pete nodded, and I continued. "But The Roost…you and Aunt Laurie…I never lived here one day in my life. Never even spent the night, not once. But, still…a part of it always felt like home. I felt anchored out here. It felt like I *belonged.*" I shook my head, thinking of those long summer days spent playing in the river, of the tiny bark boats drifting off into the unknown. "When we stopped coming out here, it was so sudden. It was like someone had cut off my arm or something—" I saw Pete wince, and I did the same. We were both thinking of that basement room. That cleaver.

"I'm sorry," I said, but Pete was already shaking his head.

"S'alright."

"That's one of the things that I never got a chance to ask Dad about. One of a million, I guess. Seems so small now, now that I know all this other shit he kept hidden from me. But when I was little, it was the hardest thing I'd ever had to deal with. It was like…it was like when Mom left us all over again. Except *we* were the ones leaving. We *were* the ones that left, right? It wasn't you and Aunt Laurie telling us we couldn't come back?"

"Nah, it wasn't us, Marcus. But, you can't put all the blame on ya daddy, neither. You gotta understand…well, you don't *gotta*, but I hope ya will. And I hope you don't think too harsh of Jim. He was doing what he thought was right. What he always did. He was putting you first, Marcus. Puttin your needs above everything else."

"The same thing Grandpa Gabe was trying to do, in other words. When he sat you guys down and told you everything."

"Yeah, but that's exactly right. It was just after Laurie caught you in the kitchen…about a week after, if I recall correctly. You probably don't remember it all too well…but it weren't just that you was trying to go downstairs. Laurie wouldn't been half so upset if that's all it was. It was the look on ya face that sent her heart runnin' like an outboard motor. She could tell you was listenin' to something. That you was hearin' something back there, back behind that door. Said it weren't exactly like you'd seen a ghost, but maybe that you'd *heard* one. Ya eyes were stuck to that door, and you had ya mouth all fixed like you was gonna say something back. You should know, Laurie hated that basement. Never did like going down there by herself. Seeing you like that, it just sorta sent the skin on her arms a prickling.

"But it wasn't till bout a week later when you and ya daddy came over here for the last time. He sent you off to go play in the Honey, and then he came in the house and talked to us." Pete leaned closer to me, his eyes locked onto mine. "I knowed ya daddy. I knowed him better than I ever knowed anyone else. And, Marcus, believe me when I tell ya, he was *scared*. Scared shitless. He said you been having nightmares all week. Said he heard you crying out in ya sleep, that he had to go in there in ya room in the middle of the night and hold you, rock you a little bit until you fell back asleep. He said you kept saying her name, over and over with ya eyes closed. 'Natalie… Natalie…Natalie.'"

Now it was my turn to feel the goosebumps ripple up and down my arms. I hadn't even known her name until today…had I? Had I heard it before, when I was younger? Had I overheard Dad and Pete talking about their long-dead aunt? And even if I had, would I have just randomly been dreaming about her? Called out her name?

No, I wouldn't have. It just didn't track.

"I…I don't know what to say to that. Wow. That's…that's really fucking weird."

"Fucking-A it was."

"So, I guess Dad had a right to be freaked out."

"Yeah, well…we tried to talk him down a bit. Mainly Laurie. Tell the truth, I was pretty freaked out my own damn self. But Jim wasn't hearin' nothin'. He kept talkin' about what Daddy had said when he sat us down. When we was kids, we believed his story. Every damn bit of it. But time has a way of smoothing the wrinkles out…pain and fear are just memories once they go away. Damn faint memories, too. We still believed about what had happened here. Those were the facts, Jack. Stuff you could look up down at the Crawford County Library if you wanted to. But the other stuff…all that shit about a curse, about that man showing up out here." He waved a hand out toward the pond. "That stuff wasn't so easy to believe the older we got. But that day when Jim came in and told us about the nightmares you was havin', it was like all them years had been ripped away. We believed again. All of it. So, when Jim said ya'll couldn't come back here anymore, said he had to keep you safe, we understood. We was gutted, but we understood."

We both stared out across the pond. We stayed silent for a long time. I wasn't seeing Dad's body floating in the pond so much anymore, and that was good. I was starting to see him as he had been. Younger than he had been when he died, back when he still smiled. Back when we'd been as close as a father and son could be. I understood him a little better now. I understood omission wasn't the same as lying, not always. That sometimes it was the only way you knew to keep someone safe. The truth can be painful—*this* had been painful. But it was a healing pain. Not the terrible agony of a knife in the gut or a stab in the back, but rather the itching and the burning of a wound getting cleaned out, of a lifelong laceration sealing itself back up.

"I'm glad I'm here now," I said. And I was. I really fucking was.

"Me too, Marcus. And I'm sorry. You know…for everything."

"No, no…thank you. Thank you for all of this, Uncle Pete. I didn't know I needed it, but I do now."

"I needed it, too. I been livin' alone with these demons for too long." He held his can out, and I tapped it with my own. I was getting back to a happy drunk, and that felt good. But there was something floating in the back of my brain like a piece of hair caught in my throat. Something irritating the soft tissue.

"There's something I don't quite understand, though."

"What's that?"

"You've brought up a curse a few times now. Is that what Grandpa Gabe thought it was? Why everything happened out here?"

"What would you call it? Bad luck?"

I shook my head. "I don't know."

"I don't either. If it was just a run of bad luck, then I'd call a spade a spade. But you ever hear of anything so awful happening to another family? Not just talkin' bout an accident or something…hell, I'm not even talking about those poor folks, God forbid, that get all wiped out in some tragedy. House fire…a car crash. A burglary gone wrong. No, ain't so simple as that, not with the Castles. Not at The Roost. If this is just bad luck, then it's some special kind I ain't never heard of. It gets passed on, generation after generation, like some kind of heart disease or diabetes or something. Something fatal. It's in our blood."

"But why here? Why this little acre of earth? What, was this place built on some Native burial ground or something?" I was joking, but only sort of.

"Nah, nothing so simple. All of America would be cursed like us if that were true…whole damn country built on a graveyard, don't you know." His voice thickened, grew hoarse, and I thought he was reaching for another cigarette in his pocket. Instead, his hand found his chin, and he scratched at the stubble there. I could tell he was picking his next words carefully—a man judging the ice before he walked across a frozen river.

"No, we ain't cursed 'cause of what was in the ground when we staked this place out, Marcus. We're cursed 'cause of what we put in the ground ourselves." He leaned forward. His words were directed at me and only me, but his eyes never left the dwindling center of the pond. "We planted a seed of evil out there. Deep in the soil. Under the water. And we been reaping its poison fruit ever since."

CHAPTER TWELVE

I started to say something—what exactly it was, I didn't know. Too many questions swirling around inside me like so much debris caught up in a tornado. But I didn't get the chance, anyway. Uncle Pete was looking off again, out toward the pond. His lips moved, but I couldn't hear any words. When he noticed me looking at him, he held his hand up.

"Hold your horses, Marcus. I know you got questions. I can see it all over ya face. I ain't sure I got all the answers, but I'll do my best, I promise you that. I got one more yarn to spin for you, and goddamit, I aim to spin it. Don't know much longer my throat's gonna last, and I gotta get all this shit out of me before it collapses on me. I ain't talked this much in a coon's age, and we ain't got enough beers left in that cooler to keep this old machinery lubricated forever."

He coughed a few times, snaked another smoke out of his shirt pocket, and lit it. The gray cloud that billowed out from his mouth rose up and met the gray, pregnant clouds above us in the smothered light of the afternoon. I didn't know for sure what time it was, but I was past caring about things like that. There was no time here, no place that existed outside of this place. It was like I was an archeologist who had stumbled upon the hidden ruins of an ancient city, a city I had never known about, had never read about, but yet, here it was; awesome in its scale, brimming with unknown treasures, resplendent in its decay. Alluring and terrifying all at once. We'd tiptoed through some of its halls, toured a few of its forgotten temples and hidden passageways. But I had a feeling we were about to go deeper into the heart of it, down where its darkest secrets had lain for so many years without being disturbed. It wasn't a good feeling, per se, but it was a compelling one. I glanced back up at the looming clouds. Storm or no storm, Uncle Pete and I were in it now. We had to go on. *Had* to.

Pete smoked for a minute or two, his eyes on the clouds as well. Finally, he looked over to me and nodded, and I nodded back. We didn't have to say how we were feeling.

"So," he said, finally. "I told you that my daddy went and talked to Grandpa Howard in prison."

"The day before he killed himself."

Pete nodded. "It wasn't exactly a happy reunion, as you can imagine, though I think they both were happy to see each other. I get the idea that Daddy went into it thinking they'd jaw a bit about what all the old man had missed out on while he was locked up. Why else would he ask him to come? But Pop Howard didn't hardly bring that up at all, side from a few niceties at the start. And he didn't want to talk about the past much, neither, least not what had happened here right before he got sent away. What Pop Howard wanted to talk about—what seemed to be the only reason he'd invited his son out—was his own childhood. The things he saw…the things he went through. Growing up here, at The Roost." Pete sighed, exhaled another cloud of gray blue smoke. "The reason," he said, "that all this shit seemed to keep happening. The reason for the curse."

He sighed a deep, heavy sigh. His body relaxed deeper into his chair, the old thing giving a sigh of its own. I held my breath, part of me knowing what he was going to say next, the other part not quite sure I was ready to hear it.

"I guess," he said, his voice full of gravel, "it's time we talked about Mr. Trench."

"So there really was a Mr. Trench?"

Pete had warned me to keep my questions to myself, but I couldn't help it. I blurted it out before I could stop myself. "I'm sorry, I—"

He looked over at me sharply, anger suddenly clouding his features, but when he caught my eye, the anger dissolved again just as suddenly.

"Yes, Marcus, there really was a Mr. Trench. You gotta let me get this out, alright?" He was still staring at me, so I nodded. "Now," he said, running a hand over his mouth and down his chin, "Hilborn ain't no stranger to tragedy, what happened out here at The Roost aside. You 'member a few years back? Hearin' about them murders took place out behind the Tooker land?"

I nodded. It had been in all the papers at the time. Kidnappings, children missing. The murderer killed, burnt up in a fire at an old forgotten schoolhouse in the woods. It was the kind of thing that was hard to forget.

Uncle Pete nodded. "Bad business that. But it weren't the first time something terrible has happened out here. Now, you gotta understand that this all happened over a hundred years ago. You go over to England or China or somewheres, a hundred years ain't hardly a drop in the bucket, barely just a few lines in their history books. But America is a young country, all things considered. And things move quick over here…only sixty years between Henry Ford's car and Neil Armstrong's rocket. A hundred years for us is just about ancient history. Long enough for everything back then to seem like some kinda tall tale. Paul Bunyan and Johnny Appleseed and all that happy-crappy horseshit." Pete leaned toward me, pointed a finger at me. "What I'm about to tell you may seem like that to you, too. But make no mistake; this all really happened. It's as true as it can be, at least. Daddy heard the lion's share of it from Pop Howard during that four hour visit they had, but other things he had to learn from the old timers still left in Hilborn when he moved back here to The Roost. It took him a long time to get the whole story. He spent years of his life lookin' for the truth. Days spent on front porches, glasses of lemonade sweating on wicker tables, watching the corn fields sway in the breeze. Nights spent down at the Hilborn Tavern, drinking piss warm beer and smoking so many cigarettes you could hardly see the person sitting on the barstool next to you. It wasn't something anybody wanted to talk about, you understand, but Daddy could be persistent if nothing else. He pulled the stories out of 'em like rotted teeth, piece by painful piece. A lot of it didn't match up, and some of it was just plain wrong, I'm sure. It'd been three decades by this point, and you know how fuzzy memories can be. Hell, I'm sure a good bit of it was just downright lies. Hard to say iffin he got the whole story. But you don't need all the pieces of a puzzle to tell what the picture is supposed to be.

"What nobody disputed is that all the trouble started in the Fall of 1910, when Pop Howard was just seven years old. Back then, little towns all over the Midwest would see a swell of people coming into town around that time of the year. Migrant workers, they call 'em now, but back then they was just hobos and drifters. Transients and train-hoppers. Men and women, whole families even, who didn't have a stake nowhere, except for wherever they were heading to next. Come over this way in the fall to pick corn and beans, then head south to Georgia or Florida to pick oranges and peaches. Hilborn always was surrounded by farms, and every year the train would bring in the workers and their families by the dozens. And somewhere, mixed in with that wave of humanity, come a man named Thaddeus Trench.

"When the workers came into Hilborn, they would set up makeshift camps just out past the town line...you know where the old elementary school is over there? Well, that was just fields back then. And for about a month or so every year, there'd be rows and rows of canvas tents and shanty shacks dotting the grass. They had everything out there: ramshackle bars set up in the back of wagons, folks selling food and whiskey and dry goods, tents for the traveling whores who'd make a buck or two at a time rolling around in dirty sheets and beds made of straw, you name it. It was like they had they own little town. Which was good, I suppose, seein' as how most of the businesses in town wouldn't let none of the workers come in. Didn't seem to be no good comin' from letting everyone mix together. There'd been..._trouble_ before. They figured just let sleeping dogs lie and all that. Still, it didn't work so well that year. The trouble came anyway."

"Trouble? What kind of trouble?"

"There was the usual sort of shit...same thing that happens anytime people congregate. Theft, mostly, but there were other things, too. Lots of fights in the camps, especially with all the homemade booze floating around. Hard-worked men pissed off 'cause they lost a hand of poker, or iffin another man looked at his woman the wrong way. Nothing too serious." He leaned forward in his chair, the hand holding his beer resting on his knees, and he was silent for a moment. He stared off to the right toward the swaying stalks of corn. Hilborn was back there, too, somewhere beyond the fields. When he spoke again, it was as if from a long-forgotten dream. "But that year, there was something else going on, Marcus." He looked over to me, his lips pursed. "That's the year people started to go missing."

"In a group like that, a mass of people comin' from all over the country, most of 'em dirt poor and far away from wherever they started, it's hard to tell exactly who went missing first or when. It wasn't unheard of for someone to just drift off during the night and never be seen again. You could do that back then…just disappear and head off down the road and nobody's the wiser. But by the time the Sheriff got called in, there were rumors of at least a half-dozen or so missing men and women. The Sheriff—Sheriff Bailey his name was, come down here from up north, up Cleveland way—he come out with one of his deputies, and they took down some names. Again, it weren't easy to just track someone down. Hell, most of the people missing didn't have no kin with 'em, and the ones reporting them gone just had a first name and a rough description to tell the law. So, the Sheriff made his reports, but nothin' really came of it. At least not until the kids started disappearing, too.

"Three kids, all children from the camps, went missing in a four-day span. Snatched up and taken away without any witnesses. *That's* when Sheriff Bailey had to start taking it seriously. Kids was different…they had folks with 'em, folks that knew everything about them, including where they slept and where they was supposed to be. Everybody was scared by then. There was search parties formed…Sheriff Bailey even called in some boys from other jurisdictions. Didn't make a damn lick of difference, though."

"Never found the kids?" I said.

Pete grunted and shook his head. "Never found none of 'em. Not hide nor hair. They did find a shoe that one of the families said belonged to their son, tossed over in a ditch about a football field away from the camps. Hell, coulda been anyone's, though. Whoever done it ain't want no one to find him, that's for sure. And it was the damndest thing, too, Marcus, with all them people livin' so close to one another. You'd think someone woulda seen something. It was like…well, it was like they all just grew wings and flew away.

"Well, anyway, since the idiots didn't find shit, they started interviewing everyone." Uncle Pete turned his head and spit out into the grass, and I saw red begin creeping up the skin of his neck and fill in his cheeks. His voice turned sharp, hard-edged with anger. "I should say," he continued, "they interviewed everyone *in the camps*. Didn't ask nobody in town. Why would they? Had to be one of *them* people, they thought, who could do such a thing. Never mind that all those lost were also workers or from the workers' families. Didn't seem to cross they mind that someone from town could do such a thing."

"They were outsiders," I said, and Uncle Pete nodded.

"Yep, that's exactly right. They was outsiders. Now, I *do* think the Sheriff and his men did what they thought was right. Not that they got nowhere with it, but I do think they tried. It was a sad business…sad all over. In the end, they found nothin'—no bodies, no suspects. People started packing up early and getting out of town, and the camp was pretty much nothin' but flattened grass and burned ground where they had they cooking fires. I don't blame 'em; it was better to leave with ya family and empty pockets than the other way around.

"Almost overnight, Hilborn was back the way it was. Well, the town itself was…the people, that was a different story. There was a queer feeling in the air, the way the workers left so suddenly. The town was like a deer carcass that had just been strung up and had all its blood drained. It looked the same as it always did, but there was something rotten inside, the muscles goin' stiff, the people cold. The work had been left unfinished, and although none of the townfolk had come to harm, the disappearances had left a bad taste in people's mouth. Ain't nothin' like that ever happened here. Emotions ran hot; the Hilborn Tavern had more than its share of fights those first couple weeks. Weren't none too happy when the dust settled and Thaddeus Trench was still seen stalking around the town, if for nothin' else than the fact he was a reminder of what had happened.

"You're probably wonderin' how the hell they even noticed him, just bein' one man by his lonesome. Easiest answer is it only took one look to know he weren't from around here. Trench was a tall, skinny man, with greasy black hair. His clothes always seemed to hang off him like a tablecloth draped over a broomstick, and his skin was pale and jaundiced, as sickly white as spoiled buttercream. Even though he came in with all them other migrant workers, nobody could recall him ever showing up at any of the farms in Crawford County to look for a paycheck. Didn't seem like he had the constitution for that sorta work anyway. Farm work is hard labor, you know, and for those drifters it was doubly so. No reason for a farmer to break his back all year—or risk injurin' his regular help—when he could just save up all the worst jobs for when laborers were cheap and plentiful. Pullin' up crops, harvesting cranberries in the bogs, and stacking bales of hay…shoveling knee-high shit out of the animal pens. It was tough work for tough men. Someone like Trench wouldn't a lasted a couple hours, and the men that saw him walkin' down Main Street at night said just as much to each other.

"Now, if his plan was to move to Hilborn, to settle down here and make a livin', then Trench didn't do himself no favors. He rubbed people the wrong way. The town has always been small, and most the people 'round here grew up here. They daddies and mommas grew up here, and they daddies and mommas grew up here. I'd say, if you go back far enough, most folk share a bloodline somewhere down the way. And they weren't too keen on outsiders comin' in and trying to make themselves familiar. You may not have noticed, Marcus, but they ain't one black family in a ten-mile radius. Even today. I think there's a couple Mexicans now, living out near Rt. 603 or something—I seen the little brown kids playing in their front yard—but you won't see none of 'em living down on Main St. You could say, 'Bunch of racist hillbillies, whaddya expect', and I guess that's true for a handful of 'em. But really, it comes down to not likin' outsiders, white or black or whatever.

Folks around here is born with a natural distrust of anything that's different. They…they don't like *change*. It's a survival thing. Just dumb animal instinct. I mean, look at the town now."

I thought about Hilborn, what little I'd seen from the windows of passing cars, driving through the small town over the years. The Roost was about a mile outside of the town proper, but even saying Hilborn had a town proper was a bit of a stretch these days. The Hilborn Tavern was still there, right at the intersection of Main and Shelby, and the Volunteer Fire Department kept its one and only firetruck in the big garage across the street, but that was just about everything Hilborn had to offer. The Farmer's Bank had shut down sometime in the '90s, the whole building demolished over a weekend, and the post office and the small sheriff outpost with its even smaller jail beside it followed suit sometime in the early aughts. The grocery store, the combo VHS tape rental place and tanning salon, even the elementary school that had been there since the '20s…it was all the same story. Different owners had tried to revive the one and only gas station over the years, but as Hilborn's population grew smaller and smaller, it just wasn't worth the expense. It was still there, but the windows were boarded up, the gas pumps removed and large steel sheets bolted down over where they stood. Had to be less than a thousand people who called the town home, now. Maybe fewer. Older two-story houses lined both sides of Main Street when you passed through. Most had flaking paint, broken down cars parked in cracked cement driveways, yards littered with sun-faded toys and busted kiddie pools. People sitting in stained t-shirts on sagging front porches or lawn chairs, smoking cigarettes and drinking beer and listening to '80s hair-metal at ear-splitting volume. I thought of the way they liked to stare, those people, of the hard looks they gave to unfamiliar cars that dared to drive through their dusty little town. Dumb animal instinct; yeah, that hit it right on the nose.

"I know what you're talking about, Uncle Pete. Doesn't seem like the friendliest place."

Pete scoffed at that. "Friendly ain't got nothin' to do with it, Marcus. They plenty friendly out here. They just poor and proud and protective of what little they have, just like any street dog with their meager pile of scraps. It's the sam—"

Pete sat forward suddenly, so quick he knocked his own beer out of his hand. It fell to the grass in front of his chair, and the pale-yellow liquid guzzled out at his feet, but he didn't seem to notice. He wasn't even looking. His eyes bulged in their sockets like someone was squeezing his throat. I thought maybe he was choking or something, or, God help us, he was having a stroke, the strain of recounting all this history finally taking its toll on his aging body. But I could see his shirt was rising and falling with regular breaths. It was just like he froze, like he was one of those animatronic animals they had at Chuck E. Cheese, one who just had their plug pulled. I went to reach for him when he leaned back in his chair. He was still staring, his eyes welded in place, and I followed his gaze out to the very center of the pond where just under half the water remained. Was there something there? Had he seen something swimming out in that green water? I couldn't tell. The gray sky cast a flat light over the pond taking away all the shine from the sun, making the surface opaque. Nothing seemed to move. I looked back to my uncle, and he hadn't moved, either. Hadn't even blinked. A cold feeling slipped down my throat and spread out in my chest.

"Uh, Uncle Pete?" I said, my voice steadier than I felt inside. "You alright?" I waved a hand. "You see something out there?"

Uncle Pete let out a long, shaky breath and then inhaled, turning his head sharply to me. His eyes were still wide open and hazy, but then they focused a bit, and he shook his head, a couple pinches of color rising to his grizzled cheeks.

"Oh," he said in a thin voice. His right hand raised up and found his throat, rubbing at it. "Oh, shit, Marcus. I'm…sorry about that. Just kinda zoned out there for a bit." He tried to laugh, but it was a broken thing. "Must'a been a goose walkin' over my grave." He coughed and cleared his throat, sat himself up a little straighter in his chair. "Now, I—"

I reached a hand out and touched his wrist lightly. "You sure you're alright, Uncle Pete?"

"Y-yeah, I'm fine, Marcus—"

"You saw something out there, didn't you? What did you see?"

"I ain't see nothin', Marcus—"

"Don't bullshit me, Uncle Pete, I saw the way you were looking—"

"Hell, Marcus, ya just as bad as ya aunt." He pulled his arm away from me, his face all red now, not just the two little spots of color. His mouth fixed in a hard sneer, and I was reminded of the few times Dad had lost his temper when I was a kid. Same narrowed eyes, same crooked jaw. If a face could ball up and make a fist, I imagine it would look the same.

"I said I'm fine, and fuck, I mean it," he spat out.

He's lying, Aunt Natalie whispered again, and my arms rippled with goosebumps.

It sounded like she was right next to me. It sounded like she was terrified.

Somehow, I stifled the scream that wanted to burst from my throat.

Uncle Pete sat up a little straighter and stared off into the fields, and I did the same. He was making quite the effort not to look at the pond again, I thought. He cleared his throat and tapped another smoke out of his crumpled pack. "Christ, Marcus," he said, around the newly-lit cigarette. "I don't mean to snap at ya. I just…I just gotta get this shit out, like I told ya. Just let me get it all out without being interrupted, okay? I just wanna get through all this shit and be done with it. That's all. Then you can ask me anything you want, alright?" His eyes bore into me, but most of that awful sneer had wilted on his face. Most of it. I nodded.

"Alright by me," I said, just to make peace. But it didn't *feel* alright. My heart was tapdancing with all the alcohol-fueled adrenaline coursing through my system, but I controlled my breathing, let all the angry, nervous energy go out a little bit with every breath. I didn't like that, the way he talked to me. Liked it almost as little as I liked the look he had given me. For a moment there, I wasn't all grown up anymore, not a 26 -year-old college graduate visiting with another adult, but just a snot-nosed kid of eight again, one who'd just been caught with his hand on the doorknob of the basement door. I felt my own face grow hot with a heady mix of embarrassment and anger, and I took a sip of my beer to try to hide it.

It didn't work. Uncle Pete's face softened, the hard ridges made by his sudden anger smoothing back out into the familiar wrinkles of a man pushing 80. His own breathing steadied, and I saw his mouth fix to say something, maybe another sorry. He didn't, and I was thankful for that.

"Anyway, Marcus, we could hem and haw over the history of Hilborn for the next few hours, but it don't really mean nothin' to what I'm tryin to tell ya. All I was aiming to say was that in a town like Hilborn, a man like Thaddeus Trench stuck out like a porcupine's quills. I told ya how he looked already, like a goddam scarecrow with half the straw gone to rot. But that weren't everything. He walked with a sort of limp, and his back was hunched over like he was a much older man. He talked funny, too. Some sort of accent… Russian or German or something, one of them rough sounding ones with all the jagged letters. Can't tell if they cursin' or prayin', you know the kind. That right there marked him as an outsider even more than the way he looked. When you look back at things, it's easy to see how things were gonna turn out sooner or later. Some things you just can't shake free from."

Uncle Pete got up then. I could almost hear his old bones cracking from where I sat. He looked down to the empty can at his feet, then to the beer I was still nursing in my hand. I had slowed down a bit, not that it mattered much after what we had already put away, but my own beer was down to the last few warm drops. I rattled it, then drank off the last sip. Pete raised an eyebrow at me.

"Empty," I said, and I tossed the can with the other dead soldiers piled up near the cooler. Uncle Pete nodded.

"Yeah, thought that might be the case. Talkin' is a thirsty business." He leaned over with a grunt and opened the lid to the cooler. "Well, shit," he said, and rose back up. "Drier than a nun's cooter in there."

I laughed and stood up. It wasn't until I moved my shoulders around a bit that I realized just how long I must have been sitting there this last time. I put my hands to my face, felt how the skin was warm and bit sensitive to the touch. The clouds had kept most of the sun off us during the morning and early afternoon, but some of it must have made it through. I'd be red as a tomato tomorrow. Already, I could feel a slight headache coming on, the way I usually get when I spend the day up at Lake Erie, the wind and the sun working together to sap every ounce of moisture out of my body. The beer didn't help, I was sure. I rolled my tongue around the inside of my cheeks. My mouth felt dry and gummy, like I'd been chewing on dead leaves. Uncle Pete was right; talking was thirsty business. Listening, too, apparently.

"Think I got some more in the fridge," Pete called out as he ambled back toward the house. I made a half-hearted attempt at telling him I was good, that I was well on my way to a killer hangover tomorrow as it was, but he just waved a hand. That was fine. Truth is, I needed another drink. Probably some food, too, something to blunt the edge of the countless beers, but that was a problem for Tomorrow Marcus to deal with.

As Pete went inside, I walked over to the water's edge. The pond was drying up, and there were at least a dozen feet of soggy, gray-green ground ringing the pond where the water used to be. More of those small bones lay about in the muck, and a few more crushed cans and other pieces of forgotten trash. The top of a rusted steel bucket rose out of the sludge, just being revealed. The detritus of days gone by. An earthy smell wafted up from that newly revealed dirt, a mustiness that spoke of life and decay and decades without seeing the sun. Not for the first time, I wondered what secrets were being revealed as the pond pulled back and exposed its soggy underbelly. If The Roost was some sort of nexus for bad luck and misfortune, then this sad, shallow pit of murky green water was the center of it. It always had been.

Are you in there, Natalie? Did you ever leave this place? I wondered. *What else is Uncle Pete hiding from me?*

I shook my head. Everything felt all jumbled up together. Too many secrets dug up for a day. Uncle Pete could only feel worse, right? Having to get through all this. All these years alone.

The wind picked up, and I closed my eyes, content to let the cooling air run over me like the touch of a thousand curious fingers. I've never been a spiritual person, but I tried to be then, tried to open my mind to any other invisible currents that might want to communicate with me. And just for a moment…did I feel something? Was there something out there? Did I feel just the slightest touch of something more substantial than the wind? Or had that just been the first cautious drops of the long-anticipated rain? I opened my eyes quickly, startled.

Just the pond in front of me, the far-off sound of someone mowing their lawn. Nothing else. If there had been something, it was gone now—gone or hiding. Waiting. I couldn't tell if that made me happy or sad.

The back door to the house slammed shut, and I turned to see Uncle

Pete coming back, a bottle of brown liquid in one hand, two plastic cups in the other. He raised them up and gave me a shit-eating grin, a little kid showing his parents the first fish he ever caught.

"Got us some reinforcements," he said, handing me a cup. He took the cap off the bottle and poured a couple fingers into my cup, then a few extra into his own. I could smell on his breath that he had already sampled the whiskey a bit before he'd come back out.

"To family," he said, and he tapped his cup to mine.

"To family," I echoed, then I took a drink, happy for the way it warmed me as it went down my throat and exploded in my chest. The adage rolled through my head. *Beer before liquor, never been sicker.* Yeah, yeah. The sick part was going to come no matter what I did. Might as well go out with a blast.

I collapsed back into my chair as Uncle Pete set the bottle down and checked the hose. He shuffled the end of it a little further into the water, a little closer to the deepest part of what was left. Satisfied, he fell back into his own chair, a pleasant, drunken grin fixed to his face. He grabbed the bottle and tipped a bit more of the whiskey into his own cup. "Alright," he said, more to himself than to me, I thought. "Alright, yeah. It's time." He nodded. He raised his cup and looked at me. "You can't choose ya family, Marcus. S'pose you know that already?"

I nodded. I did. I knew that very well. Who would choose a suicidal dad and a deadbeat mom? A bit of Uncle Pete's smile creased around the edges like an old photograph kissed by flames. He nodded back.

"Yeah, I figured you did. But just remember, blood don't make you who you are, alright? Bible says we got original sin, but I think that's horseshit. We ain't born with nothin' we can't worsh off. We ain't gotta pay for nobody's sins but our own."

It wasn't a question, but Pete stared at me as if he was waiting for an answer, so I nodded again. That satisfied him. He downed his cup of whiskey, and fidgeted a bit until he was comfortable, the bottle resting easy in his lap.

"No sin but our own," he muttered.

CHAPTER THIRTEEN

"Alright, so where was we? Oh yeah, I remember, we're getting right down to the thick of it." Uncle Pete breathed out heavily, and I was surprised to see a large plume of smoke drift up into the air. I hadn't even seen him light the cigarette this time. The whiskey was already doing its work it seemed, my mind uncoiling like a sea snake basking in warm shallows, swimming off in search of cooler waters. I cleared my own throat and sat up a bit straighter, worried that if I didn't, I might just melt into the faded fabric of my chair. Uncle Pete pointed out toward the pond, gesturing with the lit cigarette.

"This pond weren't here when Great-Grandpa James bought the place back in 1910. Does that surprise ya? You see all that gray, clumpy shit there, down in between the moss and mud? That's river clay. Pulled up from the banks of the Honey and hand-packed all along here. Whole place was different back then, really. Just a ghost of what it is now. Back in 1910, there weren't much here. There was the old barn, of course, leaning like a one-legged drunk, the one that had *Ricker's Roost* painted above the door. And, there was the original homestead, or what was left of it. Really just a pile of termite-ridden lumber by then. That woulda been back there." He pointed a thumb over his shoulder. "Pretty much right where the house is now. Don't know much 'bout the family owned this place before. Ricker, or whoever.

Don't know iffin they had a family or what, but the old house weren't more than a one-room shack. And somewhere over there—" He gestured toward the garage. "That's where the outhouse was. The Rickers, whoever they was, they'd been gone awhile by then. Hard to tell iffin they raised animals or anything. I guess there was some rotted fenceposts, but who can say. If they'd ever raised crops, then the land and rain had worshed away any sign of that too. But, at the very least, they had some kind of vegetable garden, cause right out there—" He pointed to the water again. "Right smack dab in the middle of the pond, there was an old root cellar. Most of the places 'round here had one at one time or another…weren't many ways to keep things cool back before electricity came around these parts. Took longer than you might expect, too. Shit, when Daddy was a boy, they was still using an outhouse and oil lamps out here. Not only did'ja have to shit in the snow, but you had to worry 'bout getting splinters in ya ass, too."

He let out a gravelly laugh, and it broke up into a series of coughs. He bent forward and hacked up something from deep in his chest and spit out into the grass. "Oh yeah," he said, once he caught his breath again, "yeah, you just thank ya lucky stars you never had to deal with that.

"Lots of folks had they root cellar down inside they house, but building a basement took time, and if you ain't know what'cha doin, it'd be easy to fuck it up. I saw it all the time. We'd get called in to fix what some other incompetent asshole had done—usually a relative of the poor bastard who owned the place—and lemme tell ya, you don't wanna be livin' in a place where the foundation ain't sturdy. Whole place could come down on ya head while you sleepin'. Bad way to go, that's for damn sure. So, Ricker had it right, puttin' his cellar out there in the yard. The shack ain't have no basement anyways. And from the way that cellar was built, they prolly saved themselves a bad end.

"The root cellar was 'bout eight or nine feet deep, and maybe four feet wide. There was some old timber joists down there, just as full of termite holes as them fence posts was, and the sides was lined with shelves for canned vegetables and the like. There was a wooden door laid flat on top the ground, and below it a rickety set of stairs led all the way down to the dirt floor. Whole thing weren't much bigger than a grave, I suppose. And that's what Grandpa James thought of it. Seemed to him that if you dared go down them stairs, them dirt walls would just collapse on you, bury you alive. As such, he never used it, never let the kids play down there, though they asked him to plenty times. Just like this here pond would be later, the cellar was off limits.

"Now, Marcus, take a look around here. You got the Honey over there on the left, and off on the other side, you got them fields." Uncle Pete turned to me, one eyebrow raised. "Kinda hard to tell when the water was high, but you can kind of get a sense of it now. Whatcha notice about the land in between?"

I looked over toward the river, and then I let my gaze roam slowly across the back yard and the dwindling pond. I wasn't sure what I was supposed to be seeing. I'd been staring at it all day, after all. I was about to say as much, but something told me Uncle Pete wasn't going to let me off the hook that easily. I forced myself to concentrate. I squinted my eyes against the alcohol blur. It took another minute or so, but then I got it. There was *something* there, something I hadn't ever really noticed. It was like staring at one of those Magic Eye posters, the ones where everything is all jumbled up until you fix your eyes just right. I smiled, and Pete saw it, gave me a smile of his own.

"Well?" he said. "Don't leave me hanging here, son, I'm 'bout to piss my drawers."

"It dips down here." I held my hand flat out in front of me and see-sawed it back and forth. "There's a…what do you call it? A *depression*. Like a natural depression in the land. Almost like a bowl. Huh…I never noticed that before."

"That's on account of the water. When the pond is at its fullest, the water fills in all the gaps, makes everything level. But yeah, back before this pond was here, the root cellar had been dug right at the center of the lowest point. Probably kept things cooler down there, I imagine. Kept the vegetables nice and fresh even through the hottest summer days. Must have been a bitch when it rained heavy though."

Without asking, Pete bent over and crooked his finger toward my empty Solo cup. I held it out toward him, and he tipped the whiskey bottle. He nearly filled it halfway before I pulled it back with a laugh. "Jesus, Uncle Pete," I said. "You trying to kill me or what?"

"Aww, it takes more than that to kill a Castle boy." He grinned and poured a hefty amount of liquor into his own cup. "It'll be over soon, son, then we can lay off." He raised his cup, and in a voice slightly thick but not yet slurring, he said, "Look away, Laurie, you don't need to be seeing this." He gulped down the whiskey, his face only grimacing the slightest bit at the burn of it. I was going to follow suit, but at the first few swallows some internal self-preservation mechanism made me hold back. I was fucked up, and even then, I knew it. Whiskey River, take my mind. I had been slouching, my body slowly dripping down the chair without my noticing, and I sat up again. What I really needed was to stand up, to go get some water, some ibuprofen, and maybe some food, walk around until my head cleared and then go take a shower and pass out. But I couldn't. No doubt, if I tried to stand right then, I'd be giving the grass a French kiss before I took two steps. I was beyond help; there was no way to fight it. I took another sip from my cup and surrendered.

It was getting on toward early evening by now, I didn't have to check the time on my phone to know that. The air had grown considerably cooler, and if it weren't for the gallons of alcohol running through me, I might have needed to go grab my hoodie out of the Forester. The wind had picked up, and with it the threat of rain was more potent than it had been all day. Every few minutes or so, I felt the cold kiss of an errant drop touch me on the arm or the back of my neck. It was refreshing. I leaned back and closed my eyes, right on the verge of passing out, but at the sound of Pete's voice, I opened them again, tried to blink myself awake.

"Grandpa James and Grandma Helen lived out of a wagon for two months while the house was being built. Back before cars and phones and the internet, folks had to rely on each other a lot more. You ain't have the luxury of just calling up a doctor when you was sick, or calling on a repairman or a construction crew when you needed a place to live. Iffin he had to do it all himself, coulda taken quite a while to get that house put up, but the country folk was there for each other back then. A few families pitched in, and Grandpa James was able to get the basement dug and build himself a homestead in just about two months. And once they was all settled in, him and Helen got to starting a family of they own. Hazel Marie came first, and a year later there was Lillian, or just Lily for short. After her came Howard Allen—*Pop* Howard. And that was that, the first Castle family living right here at The Roost.

"Now, I don't know too much 'bout them early years, 'cept for what I told you. The only thing I will say is Grandpa James had himself a reputation for being a mean old sunuvabitch. Seems to be the one thing that gets passed on among the Castle men, a shit-kickin, godawful temper. I'd say, if you could go back far enough, you'd find a Castle man getting drunk and raising hell on Noah's Ark. It's a wonder we made it this far, Marcus; it really is." Pete shook his head, muttered, "We're survivors, that's why. We know what we gotta do to get by, to get through the tough times." He looked down to his cup. "Even when it's hard."

Pete was drunker than he was letting on, I could see that even through my own semi-conscious state. His eyes were heavy behind his glasses, and his tongue kept flicking out and running over his dried lips. He looked old to me then, older than I'd noticed before. But why shouldn't he? I would consider it a miracle if I could still get around as good as he could when I was his age. He still stood upright, not hunched over or worn out the way some men get, especially when they've lived a life full of hard, blue-collar work the way Pete had. He was still strong. I admired him. He was right, he was a survivor, a human bridge between my present and what seemed like the oh-so-distant past. For what seemed like the 20th time that day, I was thankful to be there, not just for him, but for myself, too.

"When all that shit was going on in Hilborn, all them missing people, the three Castle kids was kinda sheltered out here. They'd heard about some of it, of course. You can't keep news like that hidden away forever, not in a place as small as Hilborn, even if you lived a mile out of town. It was all anybody was talking about that fall. And whether it was the postman and Helen jawing on at the end of the driveway, or James and the neighbor, Bert Clawson, sittin' 'round the kitchen table havin' a beer, the kids were bound to hear about it. But The Roost was its own little island, and most of the troubles drifted around it without ever actually touching the place. Life out here went on as usual. Until it didn't. Until the night the trouble come here. Until that black night when Sheriff Bailey came to visit.

CHAPTER FOURTEEN

Sheriff Bailey, 1910

The ride out to the Castle place wasn't a long one, but any ride done under the cover of darkness and just a few strokes past midnight does something to a man. Puts thoughts in their head that aren't normally there. The blackness of the night, the shadows, they come alive at that ungodly hour. Even a man with a sound mind and a confidence in their being tends to see the shapes of things unimaginable peering at him across the deep valleys of lightlessness. There have been many times since I moved from Cleveland down here to Hilborn when I was struck by how a subtle change in scenery can be disconcerting to the soul. How replacing tall buildings with miles of fields and forests can loosen the screws securing your perception of the world. Make you come untethered; a lifeboat cut from the sailing ship and sent adrift. I'm a lawman. The structure of my adult life has been built on a foundation of facts. But out here in the country, in this vast empty sea between islands of humanity, those things which I know to be true, they seem less substantial. Less concrete. These fields, these trees, these piles of rocks and dirt, they're as old as the earth itself, and in that absolute darkness beyond where the light from my lantern can reach, I know there are things living among them that are just as ancient. Things that like to stay hidden. I can feel their eyes on me as my horse plods down the road.

I am a stranger; an intruder. I do not belong.

I shiver in my saddle, hunch over a bit so as to make myself one with my horse. Perhaps those things watching from the darkness will let us pass freely if they perceive us as one entity. Perhaps they will forgive this trespass.

"You alright, Sheriff Bailey?" a voice calls from behind me, and I almost drop my lantern. One of the Ruddock boys, Slim or Stansel, I can't ever tell them apart. I clear my throat.

"Right as rain. Be even better when we get this business over with. You sure you don't want to tell me what the hell we're doing out here when all the good people are fast asleep?"

The Ruddock boy rode up alongside of me. His eyes were as wide as mine must be, the way the light is shining off of them, but I don't mention it. Speak of the devil, and he shall appear.

"Wish I could tell ya more, Sheriff, I do, but I don't fully know m'self. Honest to God. James Castle came to the house a couple hours ago, told me to come get ya, that's all. Said it was important."

"So you've been telling me."

"He had Bert Clawson with him, like I said. He seemed pretty torn up over something."

"You told me that, too."

"Right, right. Awful sorry, Sheriff, I—"

I held up a hand, cutting him off. "Don't mention it. It's not your fault." I sighed, sat up a little straighter, shadows be damned. "I'm grateful for your company."

The moon hid behind clouds, but stars poked through at intervals. Not enough to shed much light, but it was a small comfort to see them there. To break up the darkness. We rode on in silence for another twenty minutes before the Ruddock boy went on ahead of me. The road curved slightly, and then we crossed a small wooden bridge. The clattering of the hooves seemed obscenely loud in the oppressive silence of the night.

"That there's the Honey River, Sheriff," the Ruddock called back. "The Roost is just down this lane here."

The lane was just as dark as the road had been, but a tiny smudge of light shone from somewhere in the distance. For some reason, that pinprick of color sent a dagger of coldness into my heart. When I'd been in Cleveland, I'd been shot at from crooked alleyways, I'd been stabbed at in gambling dens so full of smoke you could hardly see your gun in front of you. I'd been threatened and swore at in court by men with unscrupulous associates ready to do their bidding at the drop of a hat. The jails up there teemed with people who wished death upon me. But that long, dark lane with just a flicker of light at the end unnerved me like nothing else. I couldn't rationalize it. Suddenly, I didn't feel like the Sheriff anymore, but just a man, small and powerless under the enormity of Creation. Naked and ignorant against the forces of the Unknown. But I was the Sheriff, dammit. I was the long arm of Justice. And these were my charges, these country folk, those who I swore to protect. I could not fail them in my duty.

But whatever calamity I had been expecting to see as we rounded the corner of the farmhouse and headed for the backyard, I was not prepared for what I found in front of me.

A half-dozen men, all from Hilborn, huddled around a wagon with a single lantern hung from a hook on its side. It was hard to make out the faces of the men, but I thought I recognized most of them. There was Curly Scheifer, the man who ran the Hilborn Tavern. The other Ruddock boy, Slim or Stansel. George Sexton. Tom Moon. Bert Clawson, the closest neighbor to the Castle farm. And in the middle, right up against the wagon, stood James Castle himself, his feet beside a large wooden door resting flat on the earth. A root cellar, most likely.

"Sheriff Bailey," Castle said, and I nodded, but before I could even dismount and ask what the emergency was, he reached behind him to the wagon, grabbed ahold of a large bundle wrapped in rope and burlap and yanked it from where it lay. The bundle fell heavily to the ground at his feet. A loud yell issued from one end of the bundle, and then it stretched out into a long moan of pain.

"Please," a cracked voice called out in a rough accent. "Please...someone... please help me."

"What in God's name—" I started to say, but Bert Clawson moved quickly, rushing forward toward that burlap bundle. Toward whoever was tied up in there. He drove his boot into the side of the tied-up man on the ground before I could stop him. Another scream came ripping out.

"We'll help you alright, you bastard," Bert spat. "You'll be warming yerself by the flames of Hell a'fore sunrise."

The men had all inched closer to huddle around the bundle, but they weren't trying to stop Bert. I pushed my way through them, got between Bert and the man on the ground. From inside the burlap came a fit of coughing, then the brown fabric started sprouting crimson flowers. Up close, I could see other bloody patches in the fabric, staining it from one end to the other. That cracked voice called out again.

"Please," came the cry again, "I cannot...hardly breathe."

I could feel myself breathing heavily all of the sudden. I held my hands out to either side of me, my fingers feeling so electric I half expected to see sparks at the tips of them.

"Now what is all this?" I looked from man to man, finding no answers in their faces. Drunk, if I had to guess, a bit of shame in their eyes but also defiance. None of them spoke; none of them looked away, either.

Finally, they all turned to James Castle. It was he who spoke first.

"We got, 'em, Sheriff," he said, nodding down to the tied-up man. He pointed to Bert. "Me and Bert, we got the sunuvabitch. This here's that Trench fella, the one came in with all them others. He took all them kids from the camp…took Bert's daughter, too, just tonight." He nodded up and down. "Yeah, we got 'em for ya."

"That's right," Bert chimed in. His face glowed pale as the moonlight, but his eyes were fire red. He could have been the drunkest of them all, the way the whiskey seemed to seep out of his every pore, but his words were clear. "I woke up 'bout eleven, and I knowed something ain't right, Sheriff. I just felt something's off. I checked in on the girls, and Maggie ain't in the room, her wind'er wide open, so's I grab m'gun and go runnin' outside. 'Bout halfway down the lane, I seen't a shadow and aimed the rifle. Goddam me if I weren't about to blow someone's head clean off, and thank the Lord I didn't, 'cause it was Jim—"

"One of our horses done run off, Sheriff," James Castle cut in. "I was heading over t'see iffin it went off toward Bert's place—"

Bert was nodding now, too. "I told Jim 'bout Maggie missin', and he agreed to help me look for her. Figured she couldn't'a got too far away, seeing as how I'd put her t'bed only an hour or two before. We grabbed m'wagon and headed off toward town. Jim here, he was of the mind he saw someone runnin' off in the shadows on his way to m'house. Said they looked all hunched over…that they was carryin' something heavy on they back. Well, I don't have to tell ya, Sheriff, but we been keepin' an eye on this here heathen since all them workers cleared outta town. Don't take no Wisenheimer to put two and two together." Bert lunged forward then, quick as a snake, and kicked at Trench's head. "Ol' crook-back bastard."

Everything was happening too fast. I pushed Bert back with a grunt. I must have had at least a foot and fifty pounds on him, but it wasn't easy getting him away, getting him out of kicking distance. He struggled a bit, but finally I got him to hold still, both of my hands against his wiry frame.

"Hold on, Bert, alright? Just wait a minute here. Slow down, let me take all of this in. Are you saying that this man here, this Trench, that he kidnapped Maggie tonight? Took her right out of your house?"

"That's exactly what I'm sayin', Sheriff."

Weariness fell over me like a landslide, and in that moment, I thought of the warm bed I had left Marianne in when I'd left this evening. I sighed. "How do you know, Bert? Do you have any proof of it?"

Bert spat. "Hell, the proof is all there tied up in that burlap. You've seen him around town, Sheriff. Somethin' ain't right in his head…only comin' 'round at night, hair all wild and lookin' like a damn devil."

"C'mon, Bert, you know that isn't proof of anything. Now look, I know you must be scared for your little girl. I would be, too. But you can't just go around tying people up—"

"He confessed," Bert said, and the earnestness in his voice made me shut up. I squinted at him, then over at James Castle. "Is that true, Jim? Did he confess?"

"Damn right he did." He pointed off toward in the direction of where Hilborn was. "I knowed where the bastard was holing up…just up there under the bridge on Water Street. Seen't him comin' and goin' plenty of times along where the Honey crosses through town. We took the wagon there, and that's where we found him. Got there just in time, too, from the looks of it. He was packing up his things in a knapsack."

"And then what, you asked him about the girl and he just confessed? Just like that?"

He shrugged. "Not exactly. It took some…convincing on our part, y'know, to show him how it could be ugly for him if he didn't feel like fessin' up."

"That's what I figured." I sighed again. The weariness was almost overwhelming. I looked down to the burlap sack. It pulsed a little now, the man inside trying to stretch out against the ropes binding him. I looked back up to Jim. "So, you go down there, start beating on the poor bastard until he talked, is that right? Was Maggie even there?" I looked to Bert. "Did you find your daughter down there, Bert?"

"No," Bert said, his hand rummaging through the pocket of his pants. When it came out, he held up a blue hair pin, a butterfly with a broken wing on one end. It sparkled in the light of the lamp. "He had this. Found it in his knapsack, long with some other trinkets. This here's Maggie's, I'm sure of it, Sheriff. I stake my life on it, matta'fact. Her momma got her that when she took a trip down o'er Ashland way to visit her folks."

I reached out, took the pin from his shaking hand, and held it over toward the light from the lantern. I squinted, rolled it over between my fingers. A dark brown spot, flaking a bit, stained one end of it. I rubbed a finger across it, then I held my finger even closer to the light.

"It could be blood, I suppose. Blood or dirt. Hard to tell in this light. You say you found this in Trench's belongings?"

"Well, I didn't…it was Jim here who rifled through it. I's busy makin' sure the bastard didn't run off."

To Jim, I said, "That true?"

"Yessir. Weren't the only thing in there, neither. Lots of odd things all mixed up. A small shoe, a little gold earring…a tobacco tin with initials on it that didn't have no 'T' at the end." The man scratched at his cheek. "Just about gave me the creepers. Gotta be from them others went missing, don't you think, Sheriff? Gotta be."

I grunted. "Could be," I said, handing the clip back to Bert. "Did you bring the knapsack with you? The other items you found in it?

"No sir," Jim said. "I…I threw it all in the Honey. Felt dirty just touchin' that stuff. I think…I knowed there was blood on some of it." He wiped his hands on his pants like he could still feel it on his fingers.

"I see."

I crouched downed to the blood-riddled bundle at my feet. Trench. Yeah, I remembered him. Thaddeus Trench. German, I think, if I recalled correctly. Didn't speak English that well. The man was a bit of an odd spectacle around town, so I'd had one of my deputies check him out after all the trouble, ask him some questions and go through his camp. We hadn't found any reason to believe he was responsible for the disappearances. But we hadn't found anyone else, either. Was it possible we'd missed something?

There wasn't any sound coming from beneath the burlap. In fact, I hadn't heard a single word in a few minutes. Passed out, maybe. But there was a lot of blood seeping through that thick fabric. Was he already dead?

"Alright, let's have a look at him." I started to untie the ropes binding him, and Bert rushed forward. I thought he was going to kick the man again, but he didn't. His face was as white as cotton, and his eyes were as big and red as autumn apples.

"Now, hold on, Sheriff, some of that blood was there—" He tried to put his hands out, almost as if he wanted to cover up my eyes, or block me from seeing what was underneath the burlap. I ignored him. The knots were tight, and soft whimpers rose up to me with every jerking motion, but I got the ropes untied eventually. Bert paced back and forth, back and forth.

James Castle walked closer, stood next to Bert, his hands stuffed deep in his pockets, just watching me. I could feel his eyes on me, though I didn't look up. I could sense how close they both were, though, how close all the men were.

The last of the ropes fell away, and as delicately as I could, I peeled back the fabric, taking care to grab a hold of the few spots that weren't already stained crimson. It was worse than I had imagined.

I whipped my head back, and a stinging sourness filled the back of my throat. "Goddam," I cried out, putting the crook of my elbow up to my face, trying to shield myself from the ugliness before me. The men all crowded closer around me, their feet making a tight circle.

I'd seen my share of homicides living in the city. Suicides, too, and tragic accidents. What was left of a body after plunging from one of those tall buildings. The mess in the road when someone falls beneath the wheels of a carriage. But this, this was something beyond even that.

If I hadn't heard him whimpering just a moment ago, I would have sworn under oath I was looking at a dead man. And not just a dead man, but one who had died days before. His face was a lumpy, swollen, sheet of blood from hair to neckline. His nose was destroyed, smashed completely flat. One eye socket was caved in, the bones crushed like a tin cup that had been left on railroad tracks, the other socket swollen almost completely shut, just a thin line. His mouth hung open, trying to gasp for air, and between his busted lips I could see dark gaps where teeth were missing.

"This…is not…right," Trench breathed out, biting off every word between wet, ragged breaths. There was something broken inside of him, too, the way it sounded.

Someone behind me gagged, and I looked up in time to see Curly Schiefer disappearing around the back side of the wagon to vomit into the grass there. A couple of the other men looked like they were thinking of doing the same, and I couldn't blame them. My own stomach was swirling, but I did my best to hold it off. I had to be in charge here, and it was hard to respect a man's authority when he was hurling his guts out. The other men didn't look sick though. They seemed like they might be enjoying the sight.

I felt a tremor run through me. I coughed twice, cleared my throat.

"Jesus wept. You guys damn near killed him."

James Castle spoke up. "And that woulda been a lot better than what he deserved, Sheriff. And what Bert was sayin' was true…he was bloody when we got there. Blood on his mouth and on his shirt already."

I looked straight up into his eyes. He was so close that his boots were touching mine.

"Oh, he did this to himself, did he? Is that what you want me to believe?"

"Not sayin' that, just sayin' it ain't all from us."

I grabbed a hold of the burlap, and I pulled it all the way off of the broken man. I regretted it as soon as I did. The rest of him wasn't in any better shape than his bludgeoned face. He had on a white, buttoned shirt, and it was torn and covered with mud like he had been drug through the river, his pants ripped and stained as well. The heavy scent of blood and piss and shit rose up from him. I had to lean my head back, try to catch some fresh air, afraid I was going to vomit on the poor man. Dark red stains covered the man's stomach, the crotch of his pants. His right ankle, obviously broken, hung so twisted from his leg that the foot there was nearly backwards. I asked one of the men to bring me my lantern. I held the light close, moving it over his body. When I got to his stomach, I paused.

"These are knife wounds. Five…no, six of them." I looked to Bert first, then over to Jim, but neither man offered an apology or an explanation. They didn't offer a denial either, not this time. There was a hard look in their eyes. Almost like they wanted me to say something else. Like they were daring me to. My heart sank, that sick feeling in my stomach turning at once to a heavy feeling of dread. I knew what those looks meant.

You damn fool, I thought. Oh, if I had had more sense back at the house, back when that Ruddock boy came knocking on my door. If I had only insisted on going around to Rick or Daniel's house before I rode out here. If I had only thought to bring one of my deputies, some sort of backup. But it had all been so quick, the fogginess of sleep clouding my thoughts. And now, it was too late. Too late for this battered man. Too late for me.

I stood up, surprised that my legs held me as shaky as they felt.

"What exactly did you want me to come out here for, James? Can I ask you that? You say Bert's daughter is missing, and you say that the culprit is this man at my feet. You say that he's already confessed to the deed. Well, alright, let's say that he did it. Let's say he's guilty as sin. Well, what do you want me to do about?"

"Sheriff—" Bert said, but I held a hand up. I felt my blood heating, rushing to my face, taking away the fear and the dread. My voice rose in accordance.

"And now, we have a man lying here in your backyard, looking like he got trampled by a runaway horse, and what exactly do you want me to do? You want me to throw my handcuffs on him? You want me to throw him in irons and question him? Drag another confession out of him? Do you really think this hardly-breathing corpse of a man would make it back to a cell?" My whole body was shaking now, shaking with the injustice of the whole matter. The obscenity of it all. I took my hat off and wiped the sweat from my brow, spat into the dirt. "You two damn near killed this man. You did kill him, he just doesn't know it yet." I shook my head. I looked around at the men gathered around me. "I should put each and every one of you in cuffs and haul you back into town."

"You shut up." James Castle hissed. The change in tone cooled my anger in an instant.

He looked back to the house, and I looked, too. Had a curtain fluttered in the lower window, or was it just the adrenaline coursing through me? Was someone awake in there, watching us? I didn't have time to think about it too long, because Jim was right there in front of me before I saw him take a step, a finger pointing right into my chest.

"Now, Ben," he said in a low voice, his jaw set. Gone was the nervousness he'd shown earlier. "And I s'pose it's alright that we callin' each other by our Christian names, ain't it? Good. Now, Ben, you need to understand…ain't nobody takin' this man nowhere."

The other men had moved forward, too. I stood surrounded by a half-dozen pairs of anxious, angry eyes. I took a step back, felt the wagon butt up against me. I was in the cooking pot now with the lid closed. The heat and the pressure were nearly suffocating. Christ, why hadn't I brought backup.

"We ain't bring ya out to investigate," Jim said, closing the distance my one step back had created. "We ain't bring ya out to find no justice. All these men here, see, we all got little ones, Ben. We all got families we aim to protect. We see a fox runnin' 'round the chicken coop, ya think we gotta just set back and let it take what it wants? No. No way in hell. We see a fox, we kill it, Sheriff. Simple as that. This here," he gestured toward the body at their feet. "This here animal, it ain't no different. So, no, we ain't bring you out to find no justice. We gonna get that for ourselves. What we brought you out here for, Sheriff, is just plain common courtesy." He reached out and clamped his hand down on my shoulder, and for the first time I saw how bruised and busted the knuckles were. Jim saw me lookin' at his hand and he smiled, though his eyes weren't smiling. "We wanted to let you know that y'ain't gotta worry 'bout no more people gone missin' under your watch, Ben. Ain't gotta worry a hair on your fat head that another chick gonna get killed while you s'posed to be watchin' the coop. And, just maybe, we thought it'd be good for you to know that if people start askin' questions 'bout where this sunuvabitch done gone, well…well, maybe you should think 'bout your own son and daughter before you go answerin' it. Maybe, you should think about miss Marianne, too." His smile grew a little wider. "And maybe, you'll think about how lucky you are to have men like us to do ya job for ya. And you'll keep ya mouth shut."

I opened my mouth to say something back, but no words came out. My brain was as dark and empty as the fields surrounding the farm were. My hands were fumbling at my belt, back to where my holster was on one side, my cuffs on the other, but that was just reflex. I stopped when I realized what I was doing, what the situation really was. My hands fell down to my side. I licked my lips, closed my mouth tightly. I grunted, slapped my hat against my leg, and then I shoved it back on my head, straightening it out best I could. I let my gaze linger on the face of every single man surrounding me.

"Hell with it, then," I said.

I pushed my way through the two closest men and made my way back toward my horse. When I was mounted again, I turned so I could face them all, face the whole gruesome scene. I was out in that darkness again, naked and powerless, but now it wasn't against the forces of the Unknown. It was the Known, and it was terrible.

"Justice isn't a matter of opinion. But I suspect you all know that."

My gaze lingered on the dirty faces of the men, then to the bloody spots left on the wagon bed, to the broken, bloody mess of a man left lying in the dirt. The man for whom I had no help to offer. I turned my horse back toward the lane, back toward that primeval darkness beyond where the light could reach. I called back over my shoulder.

"May God show you more mercy than you yourselves have shown this night."

And then I prodded my horse forward and let the darkness take me.

Madame, too. His smile grew a little wider. You should be a sailor, like you. I'd like you to have met her, like you to do your job, and you've had your own stuff.

I opened my mouth to say something back, but now it was empty. My chest was dark and empty as the Gulf's surface that night here. My legs were tumbled on belt back to where my belt was on one side, my cuffs on the ocean's surface that was just a little wider. When I realized what I was doing, what the situation really was, my hips fell down as my stockrail. I closed my eyes. I pictured it, pictured player language, but that I showed. Back as much as straightening in myself, until I let my legs arms on the floor of even simplening. Surrounding me.

CHAPTER FIFTEEN

Uncle Pete coughed and poured himself another drink. He held the bottle out to me, and I grabbed it, poured myself a little bit more. Things were starting to feel more than a bit fuzzy around the edges, but I could see clearly in my mind's eye everything Pete had said. I'd visited Gettysburg once with my dad when I was eleven. It had taken nearly an entire weekend to drive around between all the different battle sites. Dad was a bit of a history buff, particularly U.S. history, and he could talk for hours about the intricacies and nuances and the death statistics of nearly every battle in the Civil War. What I thought was going to be a long, boring couple of days turned out to be one of the best trips of my life. At every battle site, Dad would give me a brief summary of what had gone down there; which generals had led the charge, how long the battle lasted, which side took the worst of the casualties. He could even point out certain landmarks and tell a bit of what role they played. "You see those big boulders over there?" he'd say, "that's part of what they called the Devil's Den. That area took some heavy fire on the second day of the battle. Almost five-hundred men died right there on them rocks, Marcus. Can you picture it?" And I *could*. I could see the soldiers leaning over the tops, puffs of smoke coming up from the barrels of their rifles while their comrades lay slain across the faces of the rocks around them. It was almost a sort of magic, hearing the story while actually being at the place where it happened. It made it *real*. And that was exactly what was happening now. In fact, it had been happening all day. While Uncle Pete unwound the twisted history of The Roost, being right here, right beside the house and the poisoned pond, I could see it all.

The wind picked up, and with it came a few drops of icy rain. From far off, the distant sound of thunder came to us as if a giant herd of cattle were stampeding somewhere just over the horizon. We were still a couple of hours away from sunset, but the gray sky in the west had bruised into a deepening black, void of any color. Even the grass seemed to be a pale, lifeless green with all the life sucked out of it. Pete was pale, too, I noticed. Shrunken, somehow. Like all these stories were physical things, some essential part of him, and every word he'd spoken had been some tiny, vital piece of him irretrievably lost. I should get him inside, I thought, get him out of this cool air before the rain starts coming. He looked like a man not necessarily knocking on death's door, but maybe one who had finally made the long descent to it and was now resting on its stoop. Still, I couldn't bring myself to say the words out loud. Even as he was, there was a strength in him I didn't dare challenge.

"So, Sheriff just left Trench lying there—*here*—to die? He just…what? Turned his back on the whole thing?"

Uncle Pete gave me a queer look. There wasn't any animosity in it, no anger at the interruption of the story, just a dawning sort of recognition at seeing something he had somehow missed. It was the look, more than the words that followed, that made me feel like I was just a young, ignorant kid again.

"He ain't have no choice, one way or the other, Marcus. As harsh as it was comin' out of Grandpa James's mouth, there was a lot of truth in what he was sayin'. People was scared to death for they kids. Even after the workers left town, things never really settled down. There wasn't any arrests, no convictions. Whoever'd done those awful things was still out there running around, just as free as they had been before. Same thing happened with them Tooker murders a few years back. People need an ending. They need closure. It was the same back then. The people in Hilborn needed an ending. This weren't too far from the Old West days…not far by a long shot. And iffin there was some trouble back then, they'd hang the murderer or the horse thief right there in the town square. A bit brutal by today's standards, but there was some relief in it. A finality. You could rest easy at night knowing them that did wrong weren't prowling outside yer window. And the sheriff, for all the effort he and his men had put in on the case, they'd never brought that finality to Hilborn. In the eyes of those livin' 'round here, he'd failed them, failed his duty. And besides, he weren't stupid. He could see the writin' on the wall. Them men gathered here that night, they weren't gonna give old Trench a stern talkin'to. They wanted blood…and they aimed to have it. No, the only thing the Sheriff coulda done by getting involved was adding his blood to what was already leaking out of Thaddeus Trench. You can call it cowardice, and that ain't wrong. But I think there's a time when you gotta see the way the cards are laying and make a decision to whether you gonna fold or you gonna lose ya ass. Sheriff Bailey saw that. He folded, and he got the hell out of Dodge."

Uncle Pete leaned forward in his chair, his eyes fixed back out toward the pond. Truthfully, though, the shallow pool of sickly-looking water could have hardly been called a pond anymore. A large puddle, maybe. Enough water to get up to your ankles. I stared out there, too, not really knowing why. Something about that spot was magnetic. Was there something out there now, something that hadn't been there before? It looked different to me, and it wasn't just the alcohol in my system. I leaned forward and squinted, and then I saw it. Just past the steel bucket, two round shapes rising up above the surface of the diminishing water, as white and smooth as twin skulls. Only a couple inches shown on each, but I could already tell they were larger than any human skull. I opened my mouth to say something about it, but Pete started talking before I could. He squinted his eyes and his shoulders sagged, and he slowly started swaying side to side as he spoke.

"It weren't long after Sheriff Bailey hit the trail that Trench opened his good eye in the moonlight and stared up at the hard faces of his captors. If he was looking for mercy, he found none there."

CHAPTER SIXTEEN

Thaddeus Trench, 1910

It is the voice that wakes me. The melancholy in it.

May God show you more mercy than you yourselves have shown this night.

I try to open my eyes, but only one of them seems to be working.

Faces. All around me, above me.

Ugly faces. Mean faces.

They are not all strangers, but I know from the looks they give that they are not friends. It is written there in their countenances as surely as if chiseled into stone, like the Commandments carved into the tablets Moses brought down from Mount Sinai. Yes, that is proper; these are Old Testament faces peering down at me. Hard men toiling in a harsh world.

Fire, brimstone, sin, death.

Poisoned apples and golden calves.

Floods. Destruction. And pain, such intense, primal pain.

That antediluvian pain, created in the chaos of an earth just born, it stretches across millennia.

Now, it resides within me.

I try to speak, to say no, I am not who they think I am. That I am no devil, no fallen angel. That they are mistaken. But my throat is clogged with blood and bits of broken teeth, and the words will not come. There is no air inside my lungs. My body shakes with the effort of it.

"Roll 'im over afore he chokes himself," one of the men says. The barkeep, I think. Yes, Curly Schiefer, I recognize his mustache. There is fear in his eyes, but fear of me or for me, I cannot tell. Rough hands grip me, fingers pressing into wounded flesh, and then I am turning, rolling to my side. Someone kicks my back, and then I am vomiting onto the grass and the clay beneath me. I breathe in the night air, and though it is cool, my chest feels as if I am breathing in fire. The skinny man's blade has punctured my lungs. I can feel the steel enter me again and again with every breath, and still, I try to fill my ruined organs with air. I am being smothered with my mouth open and gasping.

"You…do not…have to do…this," I manage to say through the pain. "I take…no one."

The skinny man, Clawson, I think, he flashes forward, drives his boot into my stomach. I scream, but it comes out as a moan.

"You shut yer goddam lyin' mouth!" Clawson yells at me. The rage radiates off him in red waves. "Where is she? Where's my MAGGIE?" The fool.

I cough. Blood dribbles out over my chin. My mind forms sentences, but my body won't let me speak again, not yet.

"'Nuff of that, Bert," the bigger man says, putting an arm on Clawson's shoulder. James Castle, this one. He calls back over his shoulder, "Open up that cellar door, let's git 'im inside!"

Cellar door? My eye scans the ground, and I see the gray clay I'm lying on has been packed all around this part of the yard. Soft, spongey clay. It is the same that lined the banks of the river near my camp. I can smell the river water in it now, now that I see it for what it is. And there, just beside the wagon, is a door. Lying flat in the earth. The cellar. My heart quails at the sight of it.

One of the men bends and wrenches the door open. Hands grip me again, lift me from the ground. Pain runs through every inch of me. They haul me over to that open maw, that chasm in the earth, and I catch sight of the blackness inside.

"Hey," I say, but my voice is weak. "This is not right. This…is not right."

But no one is listening to me, not these men with their hard faces.

From above the open door, I see that even the silvery moonlight dares not pass its threshold. It is not a place where light can exist. Nor life. I try to scream, but then I am falling, falling into that deepest dark.

I have just enough time to wonder what things are concealed there, where the light cannot reach, and then my body hits the dirt floor. My broken ankle twists even further with the impact, and then I am screaming, really screaming, but the cellar holds the sound in the same way it refuses the moonlight to enter it. My body is on fire, the pain, molten lava covering every piece of me. Sweat pours off me, sweat and blood and fear, dripping into the dirt. My breath comes in short, heavy gasps. I turn my neck as much as I can to look back up. The doorway is a square of slightly-lighter blackness above me, a scattering of lonely stars peeking out of the night sky. I can no longer see the moon. Perhaps it has hidden itself in shame. But the stars were still there, bearing witness. My heart leaps at the sight of them. They will not leave me. There is salvation there, in those small pinpricks of light, the way the beam of a lighthouse is salvation to a ship lost in the night.

But then, the door is closing, and I can no longer see them.

The darkness is absolute. It consumes me.

Yelling, screaming, it is my only recourse, but even that is nigh impossible. My scream is nothing more than a thin whistle of pain. I think of where I am, this farm, this country. I think of a pig squealing in fear just as the blade of a farmer's knife slices through its throat. That is what my screaming is now, what it has been reduced to. I hear it echo around the small chamber of my captivity, and I can hear that there is no hope left in it. Only pain. Only fear.

I do not fear death; I never have. It is only natural, after all. For some, like me, Death has walked a longer, slower road to reach out its skeletal hand, to put forth its scythe and to reap a life long-lived. But, it is here now, and there is nothing natural about its arrival.

Above me, a scraping sound, then a final, heavy thudding on the wood of the door.

The sound of a casket closing. My fate sealed.

Then, silence.

There is no time in complete darkness. No reality, when opening and closing your eyes makes little difference. No sense of being, other than the pain. My mind drifts. I think of my own journey, like Death's, the long and winding route I've walked through this life. I have always felt like a foreigner, even before I came to this wretched country. Even when I could speak a common language, speak it fluently, to be able to articulate my thoughts in a way others could understand. Even then, I was an outcast, an exile. A man without a native land. Here, though, I think, it was even more pronounced. I was a pariah to this town. A leper. Enlightenment is always a thing to be feared by the ignorant. Tonight was not the first night I saw the hatred twisting the faces of my captors. I should have left this place long ago. I should have never come.

Somehow, sleep takes me. For how long, I am unsure, but it is raw fear that wakes me. It is chanting in the language of the blood that courses through me.

RISE RISE RISE RISE RISE

I listen as well as I can. Adrenaline rushes through me, sealing off some of the pain, numbing it. I struggle to get my hands beneath me, to lift myself up to a sitting position. I must get up. I must get out of here before these men come back, before they decide to hurt me more, whether with blade or fist or gun. I will not sit idly by while Death approaches. I must leave before these men kill me. I struggle to my knees, and that is when I feel the water dripping down on me from the cracks in the door above.

It's raining. I did not hear the thunder, but now it is raining. And the heavens have opened up from the sound of it.

I cannot see the water, but I can hear it rushing down to me now, down the staircase in front of me, the cold water pooling around my knees. I gasp at the chill it sends through me. I stagger up on my good foot, my hands blindly reaching then finding a wall to brace myself. The coolness of the water, it soothes my wounded ankle as it rises. There is a deep richness in its scent, a familiar mixture of earth and minerals. Like the clay, it reminds me of my camp under the bridge in town along the banks of what they call the Honey River. But this is rain, it must be. It cannot be river water, not here.

The darkness is unaffected by the presence of the water. I keep my eyes closed, hoping that by denying myself sight that my other senses will be enhanced, that by sound and touch alone I can find my way out of this hole, this grave, lead myself to safety. I stagger forward in a half-walk, half-crawl, my head burning hot with fever, every wound screaming, but still, I must go on. I must RISE.

My foot finds something in the darkness near the floor, something solid, the bottom of those wooden steps, and then I stumble. I fall to the floor, shocked at how deep the water is already, at the coldness of it. It is coming in too quickly, flowing faster and faster down those steps, rushing down them like a waterfall. Every drop a grain of sand in an hourglass. I must hurry.

My hands find the stairs again, and I pull against the current. I am so weak, the water almost takes me, almost drags me back to the rear of the cellar, but my grip does not fail, I won't let it. I grip and I pull and I strain against the water, climbing up the stairs now. Higher and higher. Grip, pull, grip, pull. When my head hits the wooden door, I stop. It has taken a small eternity, but I have reached the top. I am almost free.

I push against the door, but it does not budge. No give, not even the smallest amount. I climb up another stair, press my back against the door with my legs bent. I heave with all my dwindling strength. Still, the door does not move.

I pound against it with my fists. Fear is driving me, fear and the need to survive.

"Water coming in here! Water coming in!"

There is no answer from above. Maybe, the men have left me here to die. Maybe I am alone now. I beat at the door even harder, pounding it like the skin of a drum, hitting and hitting it in that blackness until my knuckles have split open, until I feel a dozen splinters of wood sticking out of my fingers like the needles of a cactus. But no one comes. I collapse against the stairs, the cold water rushing over me, taking with it my blood and my tears, where they will soak into the earth of the cellar.

Why was I struggling so hard for survival, when this whole life has been filled with struggle? Who was I to try and stall Death in its duty? Hadn't Death already been delayed much longer than most? A weariness overtakes me. I sigh, lean my face back so I am staring up at the door. Just beyond it, I know those stars are still there. Looking down, not with salvation any longer, but indifference. I close my eyes, indifferent now as well.

A stream of water, somehow heavier than the rest, it falls across my face, taps insistently at my forehead. I reach above me, my hand shaking. My fingers trace the gushing water back to its source. A hole. Nearly perfectly round, the size of a Morgan dollar. I almost smile. A knothole in the wood of the door, most likely pushed out from the force of the water above. I cover it with my hand, and the flow of the water into my prison cell cuts off almost completely. I do smile this time. My other hand presses on top of the first, and when I push against the wood, I can feel it give slightly. Just the barest amount, a miniscule point of weakness softened by the water. But it is something. Perhaps, Death's hand can be stayed a while longer. Perhaps, this is not the end.

I snake a finger through the hole, bending the tip around the edge. I pull. The wood is waterlogged. It sags slightly. I force another finger through, the skin tearing along the side, but I hardly notice, not even when the blood runs down my wrist. Two of my fingers are free, after all. And if two fingers, why not the rest? I grip with those two fingers and I pull and I pull, but the wood does not give any more than it has already. Scheiße. I grip the forearm of my raised hand with the other, then I pull on that, lifting myself up off the stairs, putting my whole weight behind those two fingers. The old wooden door groans. And then, the weakened wood around the hole splinters. A piece no bigger than my pinky finger breaks away.

I hold it in my hand, this small piece of wood, and I stare in wonder at it in the darkness. I laugh, I cannot help myself. I laugh and I laugh, and I realize that is not the laughter of a sane man, but I do not care. It is the laughter of a man who sees the changing of his fate.

Water gushes through the enlarged hole, an entire bathtub of it, it seems, nearly knocking me from my perch upon the steps, but I hold on, and it is over quickly. The flow of the water seeping through the other cracks in the door slows to a trickle. My fingers reach for the hole again, but I pause. I crane my neck so that I can look closer. There it is, the night sky again. Just a small piece of it, but to me, it is the entire world. The stars look back at me. Those lights, they mean freedom and they mean life, and they are not distant now, but near enough for me to hold them in my grasp. Laughter bubbles up from my punctured lungs. It sounds a little more sane now, and that gives me comfort. Soaking wet from hair to boots, soaked nearly down into my bones, I am like a man who has been baptized. And I feel that way, too, like I have been reborn. I have been cleansed. I am alive.

The hole is large enough to get three fingers through it this time, three without tearing the skin from them. I hook them through and fasten them around the edge of the hole. One more small piece, and my entire hand will be through, perhaps even my arm. I grip my forearm, same as before, and I can feel the wood already starting to break away again when the thin side of a shovel's head arcs down through the air above and slices into my exposed fingers. It cuts them straight to the bone, then through it.

There is no pain, not right away, only shock. I scream in surprise. I pull my hand down, gasping, cradle it against my chest, feel the hot blood bubbling out of each severed tip. No No NO. Damn that traitorous sky. Damn it for its false hope and its hollow promises. But when I look back up, the sky is gone, the stars blacked out once again. A face has taken its place, a face draped in shadows.

"Try that again, and you'll be missing more'n a few fingers," a voice calls down, and I know it to be Clawson. A shovel clangs against the door in warning. "Where the hell is Maggie, Trench? Just tell me what the hell you did with her!"

It is hard to find my voice, and when I do, it is stretched leather, taut and rough-sounding.

"I don't…I don't know…why…are you doing this," I rasp, every word hurting. "I have…done nothing…to you."

But the face was gone from the hole, only water and the night now filling it. Tears stream down my face. Where they find the stumps of my fingers, they burn. I am not an animal. This is not how things should be. I turn to the hole, lift my face to it, put my mouth right underneath it.

"I know no girl. I…have…no girl. Other man, he…Castle…he have blue…butterfly. In pocket. He take from pocket. Not mine. Not…mine."

The shovel comes quicker this time. I pull my head away right before it bites into the wood, before it bites into me. But it is not Clawson this time. It is the man Castle who stares down at me.

"That's horseshit," he screams into the cellar. "You a goddam liar, Trench We know what you did…we know what you did…" Other voices talking now, out there in the night. Someone pushes Castle to the side, and I tempt fate, press my face closer to the door. The others are back. Or, maybe, they never left.

These men are angry, but they know not true rage. The pain I have suffered at their hand, the indignity. Desperation can override fear, can overwhelm pain. Every breath is a stabbing cut, and every word a knife in my throat. I spit them out like daggers.

"It was you. You, Castle…not I. You with the blue butterfly. I take… nothing. I take no persons. No girls. I bother no one. You take the blue butterfly and you put…you put it in my bag and you attack…attack me. I hurt not one. I take not one."

Commotion from outside. Rumblings, getting louder. Too indistinct behind the sound of the rushing water, but I know they have heard my words. Castle's voice is the loudest, and he is nearly shouting now.

"A fox'll chew off its own paw iffin it gets caught in a trap. This ain't no different, fellas. Just tryin' to save his own skin."

Silence again. The rage, that pure, driving force, it has left me alone, like the men above have. I do not wish to look up through that hole again, to expose myself, so I wait. Eventually, Castle's face is back, peering down at me. There is murder in his eyes.

"Any man with his head in a noose would say just the same, Trench. You think God don't know what you've done? You think he ain't know you for the liar you are?"

I do not flinch at his words, nor at the murderous stare. I say nothing. More yelling outside. Castle's face slides from view as someone shoves him. Feet trample the door above, a scuffling of steps as the old wood groans, and I wait for it to break, pray for it. But it holds. Clawson again, at the hole.

"Where's my girl, Trench?" he says, and his voice cracks on the word girl. The anger from before is gone. Now, there is nothing but a thick sadness welling up in his eyes. "Please. Tell me where she is and I'll get you outta there, God as my witness, I will."

I can only shake my head.

"Please," he whispers.

"Him," I whisper back. "Not me, him."

Clawson says nothing, just stares at me. Jailor to the condemned.

Then, he lifts his head to the sky and screams. His hands pound down on the door.

"You lie!" he screams. His hands beat against the wood again and again, screaming with every hit, "You lie! You lie! You lie!"

Hands on him, an arm snaking around his chest, and he is pulled away.

I see whatever small chance of salvation I had being pulled away with him, slipping through my missing fingers. Something heavy is dropped onto the door, and it covers the hole, and I know that the sky is gone forever. Another loud sound, similar to the first. The door groans in protest, but the wood holds. I scream, I beg, I beat at the door, but the water keeps flowing down through the holes and the cracks, oblivious to my cries. There is nought to do but wait now, wait for the end. It is a short wait.

The water is not gushing down as it did before, but it is flowing fast enough. I can hear it climbing up each wooden step, getting closer to me. It is not until it reaches the third step from the top, the step where my feet are, that I begin to panic. No, no, I am not ready. One last surge of adrenaline. My cries are inarticulate now, the howl of a wild animal. I beat at the door. I scratch at it, gouge the wood with my fingers until all of my nails crack and break away from the skin, until the tips of my fingers split open and they bleed into the wood. I try again to brace my back against the door and leverage my arms and my good foot against the steps. I strain, heaving with all of my might, pushing until something pops in my lower stomach, a gunshot of pain erupting down there. Still, I push. I WILL NOT GIVE UP. As the last of my strength is leaving, I hear the cracking of wood. But it does not come from above me, it comes from below, down on the third step where my foot is planted. The old, worn-out staircase gives way with a sickening lurch. The step splinters in half, and then I am falling into the darkness, into that freezing abyss. A piece of the staircase, a shard of wood as long as my forearm, is jutting into my thigh, skewering the meat there, but that individual pain is lost in the sea of agony that runs over me. I find my feet, stand in the water that is now up to my chest. I cannot reach the ceiling, not even with my arms outstretched, not even standing on the tips of my good foot. So, I climb. I try to climb the remnants of the rotten staircase, but it breaks apart after two steps, collapses into the water around me. I am floating, my feet only skimming the ground if I extend my legs to their fullest. The water rises around me, and I rise with it, treading in it, trying to keep my head above it. Far too long, but also, far too soon, and my head is brushing the ceiling of the cellar. I tilt my head back, maneuver myself along the ceiling with my hands, searching, searching, finally finding the door, the splintered knothole. The cuts on my lips burn, but I stretch them wide around the hole, the only source of fresh air, even with it being covered on the other side. The water climbs. Over the back of my neck, over my ears, over my eyes. But then, the water, it reaches my lips, and every breath in brings more water than air, every breath possibly my last so I keep trying. Keep trying even as the last of the air is gone and the space is completely filled with water, I keep trying.

I curse this place, I think, as the water fills my lungs.

Everything dark now, everything black. Silent.

Black out the stars. Black out the night. Black out this whole godforsaken earth. If I could only dig deep enough, if I could claw my way through the soil and the bedrock, if I could burrow to the center of this doomed planet and find its monstrous heart, I know it would be as black as this cellar, as black as this night, its blood just as black and cold and dead and uncaring as this bitter water.

I. Curse. This. Place.

My lungs are filled with the metallic coldness, inside and out, and a calmness washes over me. It is not a peaceful calm, just a letting go. Not surrendering; a relinquishing. I allow my arms to stop moving, my legs to cease their kicking. I hold that black water in, and I begin to sink slowly into the depths of this drowned cellar, my own watery mausoleum. I drift down until I am lying on the floor and the whole world is above me, and everything is made of pain and loneliness and black water and silence, and I am, too.

I. Curse. This. Place.

CHAPTER SEVENTEEN

I couldn't move. Beside me, Uncle Pete slumped forward in his chair, and his shoulders gave a shudder. His head fell heavily toward his knees, and he wavered there, swaying softly from side to side, one tiny nudge away from collapsing completely into the wet grass. But still, I couldn't move. My eyes were stuck to those two round objects out in the water, now almost completely exposed to the air for the first time in a hundred years. Large, round rocks, as blank as the headstones in a pauper's cemetery. The final two nails in Thaddeus Trench's coffin. They were only as big as bowling balls, but they must have seemed like boulders, for how little he'd been able to move them. Just two ordinary rocks pulled from the Honey River; the difference between life and death.

And beneath them, the cellar door, just starting to reveal itself.

A loud, concussive clanging rang out like an air raid siren, and I lurched forward in my chair, my cup tumbling out of my lap. Uncle Pete grunted, gave out a startled yelp as he sat up, his head swiveling back and forth, his eyes two headlights stuck on the high beams. It took me a moment to realize it was the pump, kicking on, somehow, the intake hose now resting in mud rather than water, the end of the hose sucking in nothing but air, but by then Uncle Pete was already on his feet and stumbling his way across the moss-covered dirt and cracked, graying clay toward it. The ground sucked at his boots with every step, threatening to pull them right off his feet. He fell, caught himself on one knee, but then he was up again and moving toward the hose. He grabbed the hose and dragged it from where it lay over toward the cellar door. "Marcus!" he yelled above the clatter of the pump, and when I got to his side, he motioned for me to help him roll the largest stone off the old wood. I bent low, and together we pushed and pushed, and eventually it moved a few inches. A round hole, framed in a spiderweb of gray, splintered wood, peered up at us like a withered eye socket. Pete slid the end of the hose through the hole. The pump coughed a few times as it sucked at the water, the engine clattering and whining like an overheated steam boiler, and just when I thought it was going to explode it hiccupped once and then evened out. The relative silence was immediate and altogether disorienting.

"Damn thing got a mind of its own!" Uncle Pete met my eye, and we both let out a long, shaky breath, our hands on knees. Then we both laughed. It only lasted for a couple seconds, just long enough for us to remember where we were. To realize exactly what we were standing on.

"It always comes back to here, Marcus," Uncle Pete said, after a moment. He looked haggard and worn out, a thin piece of metal that's been bent and folded, heated up nearly to its melting point by flame only to be beaten flat between a hammer and a blacksmith's anvil. He looked depleted. But he did not look drunk, not anymore. His eyes were clear and bright. Boyish, almost, some queer excitement bubbling below the surface. He tapped his muddy boot against the wooden door.

"Everything always comes back to this right here. This land, this house, this square of wood sunk into the ground. Covered in water and death and a century of bad luck, but never really buried. Never forgotten." He shook his head, staring down at it thoughtfully. Then he looked up to me. "Don't look like much, do it?" He took his hat off and put his hand on his hip, shaking his head again as if to say what a shame it all was. What a tragedy. What a cruel joke. He sighed and looked out at the muddy perimeter of what used to be the small green pond. His eyes found the rusty steel bucket just a few feet away. "You know, I'm sure I ain't need to tell ya what happened after everything went down that night—that *horrible* night."

I didn't know the particulars, but I could guess. Pain. Suffering. Loss.

Uncle Pete pointed over to the house, toward the little downstairs window near the corner. "Pop Howard saw it all from right over yonder, saw every last bit of it. Heard most of it too. He ain't tell nobody. Grandpa James woulda skinned him alive iffin he had the fool sense to bring it up to him. But he never told Hazel or Lily either. So, he was surprised when he heard the girls talking the very next day, whispering to each other in the hallway outside his room. "We gotta help him," they was saying. "Gotta help the Cellar Man." Pop was horrified, as you can imagine, but what was he to do? He was only a boy…a boy who watched a man get murdered in his back yard. He just figured they'd been awake, that they'd seen the same thing he had." Uncle Pete put his hat back on.

"The next mornin', the girls was dead. Drowned, the both of em. Right out here, right above this door. Grandpa James walked out in the mornin' and stared out here, and all he saw was two pairs of small feet stickin' out the water." Uncle Pete walked over to the rusty bucket, nudged it with his foot. It didn't move. "They'd filled this old milking pail full of rocks from the river, then they strung a rope through its handle and tied each end to the other's wrists. They carried it out here together…only way they *coulda* carried it, heavy as it was. When the water was too deep to keep their heads above it, they musta kept walking with they arms up in the air. No way to know f'sure…no one saw 'em until it was too late. By the time Grandpa James waded out here, they was gone, they little bodies gone cold."

"Jesus," I breathed out. I stared at the old milking pail, and my body gave a shudder. It wasn't the cold though, or the whiskey running full throttle through my blood. It was the tragedy of everything, of all of it. One more tragedy to chalk up to the Cellar Man. One more judgement to be passed onto the Castle family. The first, it seemed, in a long line that stretched across the decades all the way to my dad, found here, right here, floating in the same forsaken waters, a hellspring whose source flowed from the death of one innocent man. I stared at the door at my feet, at the cracked wood gone soft and splintered. There was one more body to be pulled from its depths. One more ghost that needed to be set free.

"Jesus don't come here, Marcus. Maybe once, but not no more."

I looked up, startled. Where had I heard that before? Was it Pop Howard who had said that to Gabriel right before the killing in the basement? Or when Michael and Lenore had been fighting? I couldn't be sure. There'd been too much death here, too many threads of history spun out and woven together, too many loose ends that frayed and split into heartbreak and misfortune. I looked to Pete, but he hadn't seemed to notice what he'd said. He was staring at the door. No, not *at* the door, but through it.

"Great-Grandma Lucille couldn't take it—couldn't stand waking up every day and seeing the place where her little girls drowned themselves. All she could see was they little feet sticking out the water while James struggled to cut they hands free. She took off one morning without sayin' a word, neither to her husband or her little boy. And Grandpa James…well, he weren't the same after that either. He sat in a chair right over there." Uncle Pete pointed to the white cooler and the stack of empty cans lay beside our own chairs. "Sat right there with a shotgun over his lap, sunup to sundown, day in and day out. Didn't talk much. It was hard on Pop Howard, to say the least. Had to start working young…he was barely eight or nine when James would send him off to other farms during the season to help out and make a couple bucks. They scratched by, somehow, until Pop was sixteen, and he went and joined the army. Only gone about two months when Grandpa James turned that shotgun on himself." Uncle Pete looked up, his mouth set in a grimace. "And the cycle continued on, Marcus. Like a boulder pushed off a mountain, gathering snow and getting bigger as it rolls down further and further, wiping out everything in its path. Wiping out everybody along the way."

"Except for us," I said, and I felt a shiver at the words, like I was tempting fate. I licked my lips and kneeled down, a fist poised above the door of the cellar. "Except for us," I said again, and I rapped against the door three times, right next to the hose where it snaked its way through the splintered hole. "Knock on wood—"

Two things happened at once.

The hose jerked downward, cracking the softened wood further, and the pump erupted into another series of whining, clanging cries. I froze, but Uncle Pete didn't. He gripped my shoulders and pushed me backward, and I fell into the mud and rotten clay. Then he was at the pump, his hand fumbling then finding the switch on its side. It clanged a few times, each clang coming slower and slower like the last dying heartbeats of a creature who's been mortally wounded, until, finally, it sat silent.

"Wh-what was that?" I breathed out. "What happened?"

Uncle Pete was limping back to me. "Just ran out of water," he gasped out. "The hose musta just run dry." But I saw his hands were shaking. So were mine. My whole body was shaking. "But the pump, the hose—" I tried, but he cut me off.

"Just ran dry, Marcus. That's all." He gripped under my arms and pulled me up like I weighed nothing more than the empty cooler. When I was standing again, he released his grip, but I could still feel where his fingers had been pressing into my skin. I rubbed at my shoulders. In a low voice Uncle Pete said, "It's time." I didn't know if he was talking to me or himself.

He bent over toward the door and gripped one of the big rocks, and with a grunt he rolled it to the side where it fell heavily into the muck. He bent again and gritted his teeth, and then he rolled the other rock off the opposite side. He was going to open it. Open the grave of Thaddeus Trench. We were going to set his spirit free. So why did it feel so wrong?

Time grew thick and sluggish. A part of me wanted to stop him, but my legs were boneless and bloodless, my arms just skin full of unformed musculature. I could only watch. Uncle Pete wrapped two gnarled hands around the hose and pulled and pulled until the end came up out of the hole. He tossed it off to the side. The door was now free and clear, unhindered for the first time in five generations. I saw now what had been hidden under the second rock. It was a circle of steel, riveted into the wood at one side. A pull-handle. Uncle Pete reached for it, got his fingers through it, and just like that, I felt all of my senses returning at once, the muscles and bones in my body regrowing, fresh blood flowing through reborn veins. "No!" I yelled, but he was already pulling at the handle, and I knew I couldn't stop him. Couldn't change it. That's why we were here, after all. What we had been doing all day. It had to be this way; was always going to be this way. He lifted the door, and as he did, the saturated wood sagged in the middle, the planks bowing out slightly but still holding together by some miracle. He lifted it up until it stood vertically above the yawning pit of blackness below, and then it was falling toward the mud. It landed with the softest of groans.

"No," I said, not a yell this time, but a plea. The blackness of the cellar seemed to radiate upwards out of the hole, darkening the air around it. Thunder erupted above us, but I couldn't pull my eyes away from that doorway. Tears stung the corners of my eyes. They mixed with the rain that had begun to fall, but I didn't care. I welcomed the sting, the blurriness of my vision. I didn't want to see what was down there. *Who* was down there. I fell to my knees.

Uncle Pete stood at the lip of the open doorway. I was surprised to see that he, too, was crying. His face shone in the dying light of the bruised sunset. He turned to me, and the sadness in his eyes made my own tears flow faster. He waved a hand at me, the same way a mother might wave their child forward to come see inside the open casket at their father's funeral. Come and pay your respects, he seemed to be saying. I shook my head slightly, but I felt myself crawling forward anyway. With every inch I got closer, my dread grew stronger, my heart heavier. It was like I was crawling to the edge of a tall cliff. My arms and legs shook with the effort of it. But still, I crawled, drawn forward by an unseen noose wrapped around my neck.

I glanced at the underside of the open cellar door as I passed it. Dozens of long, ragged scratches covered it, deep gouges in the wood like marks left by a prisoner on the walls of his cell to count the days. Hundreds of them. If I looked close enough, would I see pieces of bloody fingernail still lodged in the wood like rusted carpet tacks? I made myself look away. When I got to the edge of the doorframe, I braced my hands against the wood and closed my eyes. Thunder broke again above us, and it seemed like the whole world was tearing itself apart. I didn't move.

That voice, that ethereal voice, called out to me again.

Leave, Marcus, Natalie said. *Leave while you still can.*

I grasped at the notion like a drowning man clutches to a life preserver. This was it, the last chance I would have to be done with all of this. I wasn't in too deep, not yet. I could leave. I could get in my Forester and drive down the gravel road, put The Roost and Uncle Pete and Hilborn far behind me. I could have, then. I *should* have. Instead, I leaned forward just the slightest and I opened my eyes.

And there he was.

Thaddeus Trench.

Most of the water had been pumped out of the root cellar, and the few feet that was left could hardly cover up the folded corpse tucked into the far corner. I saw the hair first. Long and tangled, as white as bleached bone, it nearly glowed in the darkness of the cellar. Some old fact surfaced in my mind, something about how the hair keeps growing long after a person dies, but I wasn't sure if that was true. It felt wrong, whether it was or not. Unnatural. And under the mess of ratty, tangled hair, right above the murky water, I could see something else glowing. Bone, I thought at first. Trench's skull, his spine. I squinted against the gray light. No, not bone, but skin. Somehow, it was skin. So white it was nearly invisible, fluorescent in the cavernous blackness. Pitted with a thousand wrinkles, vacuum-sealed to the skull beneath. But how could there be skin? Another fact surfaced, one I was more sure of. Cold water preserves. Prevents decomposition. There've been 1000-year-old corpses pulled from thawing tundra that looked like they died last week. Had to be it. The knowledge didn't stop my heart from galloping, didn't prevent my breath from snagging in my lungs like an errant nightmare in the web of a dreamcatcher. It was real now.

What was left of Thaddeus Trench was curled up in the corner of this godforsaken pit dug into the backyard of my ancestral home, and everything was real.

My stomach flipped, the alcohol rioting to get out, but I closed my throat and held it in. Instead, I coughed twice, felt the acid gurgling at the back of my mouth. My head swam in a sea of disconnected thoughts, and from those confused depths a single thought rose, floating to the choppy surface.

"U-uncle Pete," I said. "I…I don't understand." When he didn't reply, I continued. "Trench, he…how did you know what happened here, down there in the cellar? Pop Howard couldn't have seen…couldn't see what happened down there. N-not from the window. How did you know what he did when the door closed? R-right before it was all over? How did you know?"

I waited. The rain poured down around us; the sky ripped open. I thought for sure he wouldn't answer. Maybe he was gone, run back into the house to get out of the rain. I couldn't move my head to look, couldn't stop staring at the body in the cellar. But Uncle Pete wasn't gone. When he spoke, his voice was low and steady and surprisingly close.

"He told me, Marcus. Thaddeus Trench…he told me everything."

And then, in the dark recesses below, the corpse moved.

Trench's head tilted back slightly. The paper-thin eyelids lifted. Two shriveled pinpricks glowed like smoldering coals in the darkness above a mess of ghostly beard. Those eyes burned into me.

My vision skewed, a swirling fog as black as the shadows below circling my sight, threatening to wash over me and bury me under its weight. The strength ran out of me like cold blood down the gutters of an autopsy table. I sagged forward, nearly toppled inside the cellar, but somehow, I stayed above, my fingers tightening into a death-clutch on the wooden frame. I gagged, *tried* to throw up this time, but nothing came out. Tears burned my eyes, and I wiped them away, dared myself to stare back into that watery tomb.

Just a corpse, now, still folded into one corner of the cellar.

No red eyes staring back. Not alive. Just bones and skin.

A shadow fell over me. I turned my head to the side, looked up into the rain. Uncle Pete towered above me, as tall as a monolith. His face was obsidian, his jaw set firm. There was no sadness in his eyes, not anymore. Not even the veil of drunkenness.

Only resolve. A man decided.

"We're all that's left, Marcus. Just us. Ya daddy broke his promise. We wasn't supposed to carry on this bloodline. We was 'sposed to let this curse die with us."

In my head, I could see arms more bone than flesh unfolding below me. Bony shoulders shifting beneath tattered cloth. A butterfly's wings cracking open the walls of its cocoon. I had to look again to be sure, to be certain it was still just a corpse.

"Ya daddy broke his promise, and then it broke him."

Uncle Pete's boots slid forward in the mud and clay. Close enough now I felt the tips of them touching the bottoms of my own shoes as I lay there.

"I loved James. I didn't want to have to bring him back here. I didn't. But he broke his promise, Marcus…what was I to do? See, he thought he could change his destiny—*our* destiny—by moving away. That he wouldn't hear the voice of Thaddeus Trench no more if he put some miles in between himself and this place. But he was wrong, Marcus. He had poison in his blood, same as me. You ain't curin' that by runnin' away. And when I called James back that last time, when he come out here, I saw it in his eyes that he was too old to keep runnin'. Too weak. Too tired. But you know what? He surprised me. I held my shotgun, and I watched him wade out into that water with that pistol in his hand. I watched his eyes. And you know what I think? I think he *did* fight it, right at the end. I saw his eyes clear. He turned to me, to where I was standing on the bank, the gun already stuffed into his mouth. I saw his eyes, Marcus. I think he kilt himself to protect *you*. You and me. Like maybe if he sacrificed his own life that it could be over. All this shit could be done with." Uncle Pete sighed heavily, Atlas finally letting the world fall from his shoulders. "Didn't work, of course. But that was James, the big brother to the end. The protector. Damn fool."

Uncle Pete sighed heavily again. This time, it sounded like the thunder.

"Now, it's gotta end, Marcus. End right here, with you and me. I been livin' with these ghosts for too long, tryin' to shoulder it all myself. Tryin' to hold it all back. Ya daddy was s'posed to help me, help me finish it. Help to end it. But he ain't hold up his half. Not until I made him. I…I can't do it no more, ya hear me? I'm old…I can't carry it all no more."

Something cold and hard pressed itself into the back of my head. I thought of that cleaver Lenore held against Grandpa Gabe's head when they were down in the basement. Then I heard the metallic click of the slide of a handgun being ratcheted opened and closed. Uncle Pete spoke. His voice was right next to my ear.

"Look down there, Marcus. Look down at the Castle family's original sin."

I shook my head. No, I wasn't going to look. I'd seen enough. The barrel of the pistol pressed harder into my skull, forcing me to face down into that blackness. Making me look at those old bones.

"See how he looks at us, Marcus?" Uncle Pete whispered. "See how he looks right through ya? I see him every night, ya know. Every goddam night since Laurie died. I think, at the end, she saw him, too. I think she was grateful she was leavin'. Even through the pain while that cancer ate her stomach, I think she was grateful, I really do." He was crying softly now. The barrel of the pistol quivered against my head. "It has to stop with us. You see that, right? All this pain, all this hurting. I can't carry it all no more. And I can't let *him* hurt you, too. I can't."

"So, so, y-you're the one that's going to do the hurting? You're going to what…you're going to kill me out here, Uncle Pete?"

"No. No, not kill. I'm going to save you, Marcus. This ain't no kinda life to be livin'. There's debts that need to be paid."

"B-but you said, you said we didn't have to pay for anyone's sins but our own, Uncle Pete. Y-you told me that. We didn't put him down there, me and you. We didn't cause all this."

"I said a lot of things, Marcus. No fool like an old fool, ya remember that one? Part of me was hopin' it wouldn't come to this. But, I knew…I knew it had to be this way. I've known it since Daddy sat me and Jim down and told us everythin'. Look at him down there. He wants *blood*. Look how hungry he is. Look at the way he licks his lips. Like God in the Old Testament, *he* demands sacrifice. That's how he's survived this long. But once we gone, ain't no one left to keep feedin' him. Once we gone, he won't have no choice but to leave, too. Leave or starve. And when he leaves, all our kin, they can rest easy again. We like Jesus on the cross, you and me. We're payin' for all they sins with our own blood. We're settin' them free, don't ya see that? We're settin' them all free."

I looked at the pile of withered bones and peeling skin in the bottom of the root cellar and a tremendous sadness fell over me. He was crazy. My poor Uncle Pete had gone insane. Left alone out here, living with all these old memories. All these decades of pain compounded. The land here was saturated with blood and grief and pain. So much pain. I'd seen the shade of my dad floating out in the pond a hundred times before I'd ever had the guts to come back to The Roost. But Uncle Pete had never left. He lived with it. The radiation from a nuclear fallout can last for decades, make the miles and miles of soil around it uninhabitable, and any living creature unfortunate enough to make their home within that poisoned landscape inevitably succumbs to the damage left behind. It wasn't any different for Uncle Pete. He'd been living right at Ground Zero his whole life. It had seeped inside of him, that poison, little by little over the years. It had gotten inside his brain and made a home there. And he wasn't the first. I thought of Pop Howard, just a little boy, growing up and knowing the terrible things that had been done here. Of Grandma Lenore, and Michael, and Natalie. Of Grandpa Gabe, trying in his own way to make things right, to finally end the cycle. But the actions of Great-Great-Grandpa James had salted the land here, and a century later, there was no chance of anything good growing from this cursed soil. Uncle Pete had tried, too, hadn't he? At least at the beginning. He and Aunt Laurie had given me some of the best memories of my childhood, right here where good memories had no place. He had tried to work the dirt, to get it to produce something positive. But he was old now, old and tired, and the weight of it all was crushing him. *Had* crushed him. Maybe he was right to want to end it all. Maybe it would be okay to help him do it.

I thought of Pop Howard, drowning his only daughter. Yelling, *This time gonna pay for all?*

I thought of my dad, water to his waist, the gun in his mouth, tear-filled eyes staring at his brother on the shore, thinking, *This time gonna pay for all?*

Would it ever be enough? *Could* it ever truly be enough?

I bent further over that open cellar. That grave. I let my body hang over the darkness, and I prayed. *Let it be enough this time. Let this time pay for all.*

"D-do it, then, Uncle Pete. I'm ready. Let's…let's finish it."

Uncle Pete raised back up, the gun shaking now, but never leaving my head. The rain poured down around us, but I could hear the soft sobs coming from the man I loved as much as my own father.

"I'm so sorry, Marcus. So sorry it come to this. But you was born into this…and only death can save you—"

Move, Marcus. Move NOW!

It came to me like the voice from earlier, but it wasn't Natalie this time.

It was my dad.

I moved.

The gunshot rang out beside my head, bursting my eardrum. The heat of it scorched my cheek. I fell to the side, and, cursing, Uncle Pete pushed forward with his hands, tried to push me into that empty grave. Instead of my shoulders, his hands met air, and he stumbled forward. Not much, really, only a couple of steps. But it was enough. I turned, gripped his suspenders in both hands. I yanked as hard as I could muster. He tilted forward, teetered on the edge. Then he was falling. He yelled something I couldn't understand. Some curse. I let go of him as he fell. But the old man had one more trick. His left boot kicked out as he flew over me, and it caught the back of my head. It was like getting hit with a brick. Everything went black. Then I was falling, too.

WHEN I CAME TO, I was lying next to the door at the bottom of the pond. The rain poured down now. No stars to be seen. The sky was a sea of blackness. I lay on my back for a long time, chest rising and falling automatically, every breath a blessing, every ounce of throbbing pain a reminder of the miracle of being alive.

I don't know how long I lay there, letting the rain wash over me. If I sat up, if I looked around at the drained pond, at the empty lawn chairs, then I would be forced to understand that it was all real. That it had really happened. That my Uncle Pete had tried to kill me. The throbbing pain in my head from the kick told me it was, as did the deafness in my right ear. But if I just kept laying here, kept letting the rain fall down on me…

A sound rose up from the cellar below me. A coughing, hacking sound. A splashing.

My insides turned cold. Uncle Pete. The gun.

But then a voice called out from the depths. A voice as soft and as light as cotton. It was not the voice of my uncle. It was the voice of my father again.

"Marcus," he said.

My heart squeezed painfully at the sound of it. Tears welled up and ran down my face. I rolled over in the mud and the old clay. My hands found the edge of the doorframe.

"Dad?"

I crawled closer.

"Marcus," Dad said again. "My boy. Come see…come see what you've done."

I looked over the edge.

Below, the corpse of Thaddeus Trench stood. The water came up nearly to his knees. He turned his face to the falling rain and swayed under its influence. Every bit of his flesh was wrinkled from the water and glowing white, almost transparent, pulled thin and taut over the sunken hollows of his shriveled body. His hair hung long and ratty, not so much white as completely devoid of color, same as his beard. His hands curled into claws, the fingers ending in roughhewn stumps, any fragments of fingernail remaining just jagged splinters. His eyes glowed in the stormy light. As I watched, the corners of his mouth lifted slightly; the rictus grin of a man long dead.

Marcus, my dad's voice came to me again.

And the corpse smiled.

Marcus, I'm so scared. It's so dark down here. He's coming for me, Natalie's voice said.

And the corpse smiled even wider.

Jump, a new voice said. The consonants were clipped, some ancient accent lilting the word. The voice of Thaddeus Trench. *Jump down, and come to me, Marcus.*

Down, into the darkness. Down, to the end.

And I wanted to. I'd been wanting to for a long, long time.

I thought of all these years of sadness that brought me here, all the loneliness. The pain. The drinking and the pills and the pulling away from anyone who cared about me. The idle thoughts of what it would feel like to put the barrel of a gun inside my mouth, just like Dad did. Wondering what it would be like to finally let go of it all. The morbid hope I found there inside those dark thoughts. The comfort. The finality. The peace.

It was all right there, right down there at the bottom of the cellar. And I wanted it.

But then, I saw the other body in the cellar. Crumpled in the corner.

Uncle Pete had fallen head-first right into that hard ground. His skull had caved in on one side, but, somehow, his glasses had stayed on his face. He looked like he was sleeping. He looked like he had finally found his own peace.

This time gonna pay for all?

No. Nothing could pay for those old sins. No amount of blood was going to wash them away.

"You've taken enough," I called down to the corpse of Thaddeus Trench. "My family has paid their dues."

I closed my eyes.

"You don't get to take anymore."

When I opened my eyes again, the Cellar Man was gone.

Just bones, now. Old, rotten bones and pale skin, lying in a pool of dirty water.

I cocked my good ear up to the thunderous sky, and I listened. Natalie was silent. My father was silent, too. I could hear the falling rain spatter in the mud around me, the wind whipping through the waving stalks of corn. But they were no longer whispering that I was home. They were saying something different now.

They whispered, *You are free.*

My Forester wasn't big enough, but luckily the keys to Uncle Pete's work truck were on the hanger by the door inside the house. It took over an hour to load all the bags of concrete mix from the garage into the bed.

I backed the truck up through the yard. It was nearly pitch black out, and the storm had turned the grass of the backyard into a swampy mess, but the truck had no problem navigating the mud. I stopped with the tailgate right above the open maw of the cellar door.

I wasn't surprised to see the pair of glowing eyes staring up at me from that darkness.

I paid them no mind.

There were twenty-six bags of quick-setting concrete mix in all. I tilted each one out over the doorway, and I cut them open with a pocketknife, letting the gray granules fall into the abyss. It took a long time. I took many breaks to calm my shaking hands, to wipe the tears out of my eyes. By the time I was done, the eastern sky was turning from black to gray, and the dark, muddled water below had risen considerably from the rain. When I finished, I threw the empty bags down into the old root cellar along with the cooler, the empty cans, the old pump. I parked the truck back in the driveway, then I hung the key in the house and locked the doors.

The rain did most of the work. By the time I closed the door, the cellar was nearly full. I returned the two large rocks to their place atop the wood. Two blank headstones for the unmarked graves below.

Trench was gone now, buried beneath a ton of concrete. Uncle Pete was down there, too. I wished I could pull him out of that grave, to give him a proper burial out at the Oakland Cemetery Bailey so he could rest beside Aunt Laurie, but I couldn't. A part of me knew this was where he wanted to be, anyway. *You're standing guard over The Roost now, Uncle Pete*, I thought, and the words rang true. I felt him there, right there beside me. He was keeping an eternal vigil against the evils in this world, now. The very last casualty in the long and bloody battle for the souls of the Castle clan.

I waited another hour or so, long enough for the morning sun to peek out of the clouds, and for the concrete to start to set. Long enough to see clearly everything that had happened here on this godforsaken patch of land. The good *and* the bad. The heartache. The loss. But there had been love here, too, once. Maybe there could be again, one day.

The old spigot at the edge of the pond whined when I turned it, the old pipe shaking and groaning, but soon, the water of the Honey River was flowing out onto the clay of the pond's belly, taking up its old home in the depression in the backyard. I sat in the lawn chair at the edge of the grass, taking sips from the discarded whiskey bottle, watching it fill. I took a drink for Dad, for Uncle Pete and Aunt Laurie, for Grandpa Gabe, and Michael, and Natalie. I took a drink for every member of the Castle family that had been touched by the evil that had been done here. I even took a drink for the long-dead, long-drowned, Thaddeus Trench. I did not take a drink for my Great-Great-Grandpa James.

There were no voices on the wind any longer. The Roost was finally at rest.

I drank and watched the pond fill, and I smiled at the sounds of the birds in the woods greeting the new day.

I didn't sleep.

I wasn't sure I'd ever sleep again.

EPILOGUE

Can a house be a ghost? Can a place?

I thought so, once, when I first spotted that old farmhouse at the end of the gravel driveway off of Crayton Road. After all, The Roost had haunted me for so many years. Haunted my whole bloodline. But looking back now, I don't believe that anymore. A house is meant for the living. It's meant to hold life, not death. No, it's the people who are the ghosts. The living people who do the haunting. Our histories follow us around. They're always just behind us. And no matter how hard we try to run, they're always there. Never far enough behind to be completely forgotten. We drag them around from place to place, from year to year, from relationship to relationship. They weigh us down, but we grow stronger from the weight, strong enough to not notice the gentle pulling like tiny anchors secured around our ankles. We carry that weight with us to the grave, and when they bury us, those anchors, they secure themselves to those who we loved, to those who loved us, to those we hated.

Sometimes, the weight of our history is enough to drag us down.

Sometimes, it's enough to drown us.

I think of Uncle Pete often. His kindness. His resolve.

I dream of The Roost.

Sometimes, I see red eyes glowing in the darkness of my bedroom.

But I've cut those anchor lines free from around my ankles. I've removed them from my father, and his father, and his father before him, at least the best I could.

I've set them all free, just like Uncle Pete said we should.

I've finally set them all free.

ACKNOWLEDGEMENTS

They say no man is an island, and in the same sense, neither is any book. While my name graces the front cover, there are many others who's influence and dedication is written into every page. First and foremost, I'd like to thank Third Estate Books for bringing this dark little piece of Ohio to life. They saw something in the story, and they helped me refine it, and for that, I'm supremely grateful. Jacy Morris, with his excellent editorial skills, zeroed in on the true heart of the story from the very beginning, and without his insight I wouldn't have been able to pull it up from the depths of the swamp. And Aquino Loayza, who understood the dark places shown within these pages, and who recognized the basement they crawled out of. Forever in her debt.

Todd Keisling created the gorgeous cover; it only took a few minutes of talking for him to completely understand our vision. He took our ideas and elevated them exponentially, and I couldn't be more floored by the results. A huge thank you to Clay McCleod Chapman, Laurel Hightower, Erika T Wurth, and all the other authors, who, despite having their own lives and demanding writing schedules, took the time to read my story and graciously share their kind words. To James Noser, who spent a Fall day driving for hours through the backroads of Ohio just to grab some inspirational photos of my hometown, and to my stepfather, Jim Schiefer, who offered to play tour guide. To my father, David Bond, who listens to me drone on and on about whatever I'm writing, and to all my friends and family who have offered so much support and encouragement through the long, lonely hours spent bent over a keyboard.

To my kids, Kailie, Oliver, and Milo, who keep me grounded, and who constantly remind me of what's truly important in my life.

And to my wife, Emily Makanani, always. Through this life and the next; all good things come through you, my darling.

In Memory of Cynthia Louise Cox,

1961-2013

THE MONOLOGIST
By Aquino Loayza

What's life without risk?

At least that's what Patrick Gallagher tells himself as he arrives in Las Vegas at the peak of the Cold War with a dream that can't be bought in gold or jewels: To become a standup comedian, a monologist. But nobody can run away from their past, no matter how bright their future may seem. The world isn't as clear as it appears. Will Patrick succeed? Or will he discover that everything has its price and some costs can't be quantified in a dollar bill?

In this queer revolutionary imagining of 1963 Las Vegas, Aquino Loayza, Author of the Queer Cosmic Epic: Deep, explores the seedy underbelly of Sin City in its infancy as Patrick Gallagher embarks on his quest to defy the odds and become The Monologist.

BURY MY HEART WITH A KEYBOARD
By Jacy Morris

Jacy Morris' collection is an assault on Indigenous identity and stereotypes, an exploration of what it means to be Indigenous in a world where identity is commercialized and weaponized. 13 stories of the past, present, and future, all exploring different aspects of our world. At times brutal, at times hauntingly nostalgic, Bury My Heart with a Keyboard refuses to pull punches and revels in its gruesome truths. Filled with callous gods, broken souls, and a constant rejection of the status quo, Bury My Heart with a Keyboard is all you can handle and more.

Christopher Bond is an author, a husband, a father, a thrift store archaeologist, and a used bookstore explorer. He may or may not get into heated air guitar battles after having one too many glasses of scotch. His short fiction has been included in over a dozen anthologies and magazines from a variety of publishers around the world. His debut novella, *The Devil Came Down the Mountain*, was an Amazon and Barnes & Noble bestseller. He currently lives in the shadow of the Rocky Mountains, at least until the winter winds drive him back to a beach somewhere.